SHERLOCK HOLMES MYSTERY MAGAZINE

#13 (VOLUME 5 NUMBER 3)　　　　　May/June 2014

Sherlock Holmes Mystery Magazine #13 (Vol. 5, No. 3) is copyright © 2014 by Wildside Press LLC. All rights reserved. Visit us at wildsidemagazines.com.

"...BUT WATSON, YOU CAN'T UNFRIEND ME."

Publisher: John Betancourt
Editor: Marvin Kaye
Assistant Editors: Steve Coupe, Sam Cooper

Sherlock Holmes Mystery Magazine is published by Wildside Press, LLC. Single copies: $10.00 + $3.00 postage. U.S. subscriptions: $59.95 (postage paid) for the next 6 issues in the U.S.A., from: Wildside Press LLC, Subscription Dept. 9710 Traville Gateway Dr., #234; Rockville MD 20850. International subscriptions: see our web site at www.wildsidemagazines.com. Available as an ebook through all major ebook etailers, or our web site, www.wildsidemagazines.com.

The Sherlock Holmes characters created by Sir Arthur Conan Doyle are used by permission of Conan Doyle Estate Ltd., www.conandoyleestate.co.uk.

FROM WATSON'S SCRAPBOOK

It was not easy convincing Holmes to let me release, after all these many years, information of a highly personal nature, but at length he relented, though with one condition. You see, *The Adventure of the Nine Hole League,* which John J. White has faithfully reported from my original notes, reveals one of my ratiocinative friend's few secrets. The case itself is an excellent one, as I have often argued, to which he customarily replies, "Then tell about it, but leave out—well, you know what."

I suppose I have pestered him about this for so very long that he has finally acquiesced just to stop what he has termed "a perennial persecution, Watson!" Truly, I cannot see why he ever minded being shown in an utterly human light, but suffice it to say that it *did* bother him, and that is that.

The condition he has imposed is an easy one; he insisted on this issue's Holmesian adventure being *The Adventure of the Dying Detective,* presumably because it shows me off as slightly less than professionally competent, but I would have defied any other "medico" to render a differing diagnosis. So there!

I am pleased that this issue of *Sherlock Holmes Mystery Magazine* includes Dan Andriacco's examination of Holmes's ongoing relationship to journalists. I don't recollect any other look at that aspect of my friend's investigative procedures, but I may be wrong about that. At any rate, it is well worth a look-see.

And now I turn this forum over to my colleague, Mr Kaye.

—John H. Watson, M. D.

✗   ✗   ✗   ✗

What a rich issue this is! Several of our continuing contributors are aboard, including William E. Chambers, Janice Law, Gary Lovisi, and my dear friend Marc Bilgrey, who is SHMM's resident cartoonist, having produced several cartoon books, including *The Private Eye Cartoon Book, The Science Fiction Cartoon Book,* and *The Sherlock Holmes Cartoon Book.* In this issue, Marc has also sent us one of his new crime stories.

I am always very pleased to offer a new Kelly Locke mystery. Kelly, a TV journalist, and her Chief of Detectives father Matt have a habit of wrestling with criminal cases that always remind one of Sherlock Holmes. This time, they investigate *The Speckled Bandanna.*

Our first-timers include Laird Long – one of a series of short shorts that will appear in subsequent issues of SHMM, as well as Gordon Linzner, and J. P. Seewald.

Our upcoming issue will welcome back Jack Grochot, Adam McFarlane, and Stan Trybulski, and the 15th issue in the works will again be an all-Holmes magazine!

We are still in need of new articles about anything criminous you'd like to write about. Articles about Conan Doyle, Sherlock Holmes, Dr Watson, et cetera, are always welcome, as are those about Rex Stout and Nero Wolfe, or any other famous mystery writer. General crime is always welcome, too.

If you have an idea for an article, please query us at marvinnkaye@yahoo.com.

(Do note there are two n's in the address.)

—Canonically yours,
Marvin Kaye

COMING NEXT TIME...

**STORIES! ARTICLES!
SHERLOCK HOLMES & DR. WATSON!**

Sherlock Holmes Mystery Magazine #14
is just a few months away...watch for it!

Not a subscriber yet?
Send $59.95 for 6 issues (postage paid in the U.S.) to:

Wildside Press LLC
Attn: Subscription Dept.
9710 Traville Gateway Dr. #234
Rockville MD 20850

You can also subscribe online at
www.wildsidemagazines.com

SCREEN OF THE CRIME

by Lenny Picker

TEN LITTLE PIPS: THE CINEMATIC SHERLOCK HOLMES AND THE *AND THEN THERE WERE NONE* TROPE

2015 will mark the 125th anniversary of the birth of Agatha Christie, the only serious rival to Arthur Conan Doyle for the title of the best-known author of mystery fiction. The occasion is being marked by several developments—fall 2014 will see the publication of an as-yet untitled new Hercule Poirot novel by British author Sophie Hannah, authorized by the Christie Estate and the first Poirot pastiche, and the airing in the US of the final five episodes of the popular David Suchet series, including the detective's final case, *Curtain*, whose publication garnered Poirot front-page coverage in *The New York Times*.

But the Poirot stories, which established the gathering-of-the-suspects ending beloved by traditional mystery authors, including Rex Stout, as the great Belgian sleuth displayed the results of his little gray cells, are not Christie's best-known or best-selling work. That distinction goes to the novel known today as *Ten Little Indians* or *And Then There Were None*, a book that scared me when I read it as a thirteen-year-old, and which has reportedly sold a mind-blowing 100 million copies. The plot is familiar even to those who've never read it—ten strangers, trapped on an island by a mad killer, are picked off, one by one. Popularity aside, it truly rates consideration as one of Christie's cleverest; it's certainly the most atmospheric, and while she plays fair with the reader, not one in a thousand will solve the puzzle without just guessing.

While some authors resort to multiple corpses to sustain interest in a lagging plot, Christie ratcheted up the tension by having her reader wonder who will be murdered next (and how) rather than if anyone else would perish. With the characters themselves aware at an early juncture that they all are being targeted for death, the author's skills at portraying what the Holmesian Jeeves has called "the psychology of the individual," have a lot of opportunity to display themselves. But what *Ten Little Indians* does not have (and does not suffer for the absence in the slightest) is a master sleuth.

N.B.: Somewhere in the clutter in which I live, there is a worn and battered box with my name magic-markered on the lid. It is crammed with papers, nearly all of which are attempts at fiction (for which a literate world is not yet prepared), including "And Then There Were None?" a revisionist look at the novel through the eyes of a certain Baker Street consulting detective.

But the insertion of a classic Golden Age rationalist into a *Ten Little Indians* plotline has seemed a natural for others. Intriguingly, the concept appeared, if not necessarily for the first time, not long before the 1939 publication of Christie's book.

Six years earlier, in 1933, Sono Art-World Pictures distributed *A Study in Scarlet*, a seventy-one-minute film that owed next-to-nothing to the novel of that name, apart from a familiar deduction about the killer's appearance and taste in cigars. Available online, and as part of multi-disk DVD collections that include a potpourri of obscure Sherlockiana, it's a bit creaky, but still entertaining—that is, if it's taken on its own terms and not compared with the legion of better screen depictions of Holmes and Watson.

For many Sherlockians, the film is best-known because the low-key actor in the lead, Reginald Owen, was the first to have also played Watson (in the 1932 Clive Brook *Sherlock Holmes*, an adaptation of the Gillette play). Owen, whose career included parts in both *Mrs. Miniver* and *Mary Poppins*, is remembered mostly for his Ebenezer Scrooge, but he does an adequate job as Holmes, even if he's the wrong physical type for the part. But the acting isn't the most memorable aspect of the 1933 movie; that distinction belongs to the plot. The screenplay by Robert Florey tosses in a bunch of characters with Canonical names—Forrester, Merridew, and even Jabez Wilson, and opens dramatically, with the discovery of a corpse in a railway carriage at Victoria Station. The dead man is James Murphy, and he proves to be just the first victim of a killer targeting members of a tontine. That group is led by Thaddeus Merridew, here described as London's Milverton-like master blackmailer. And, as in the Christie story, verses of the Ten Little Indians nursery rhyme (starting with "Six little black boys playing with a hive; a bumble-bee stung one, and then there were five.") seem to parallel the murders. Intriguingly, an aspect of the solution anticipates the answer to Christie's puzzle, although there's no reason at all to believe the film had any influence on her. And even if it did, there's no comparison with a B- B (pun unintended) movie that doesn't sweat the details (221A Baker Street, anyone?) and a carefully-constructed classic that will still be enjoyed, long into the future.

But the better-known introduction of Holmes into a *Ten Little Indians* plotline is 1945's *The House of Fear*, one of the Rathbone/Bruce films. Along with the other eight in the Universal series that do not involve the Nazis as bad guys, *The House of Fear* starts very strongly. An off-screen narrator recounts the grim doings at Drearcliffe House, in Scotland. The structure has been the subject of a legendary curse for generations—it is said that at Drearcliffe, "no man goes whole to his grave."

Drearcliffe, which is the ancestral home of Bruce Alistair, currently houses the seven members of a fellowship known as the Good Comrades. Their lives there have been unremarkable despite the legend, until the arrival one evening of an envelope addressed to retired barrister Ralph King.

As the narrator recounts, "King received it casually. When they saw the contents, the Good Comrades took the whole thing as a joke but their housekeeper was right, it was no laughing matter."

Those contents were seven orange pips, and as in the canonical "The Five Orange Pips," the seeds are heralds of death. The night after the pips were set on King, he died in a fiery car crash over the cliffs near his home. An untimely end is also in store for Stanley

Raeburn, an elderly actor, after the Mrs. Danvers-like housekeeper hands him an envelope containing six orange pips. It's after Raeburn's death by drowning (somehow, presumably getting maimed in the process to keep faith with the curse) that the narrator, who turns out to be an insurance agent named Chalmers travels, to 221B for assistance.

But Holmes and Watson's arrival on the scene—and even the eventual presence of the one man who makes Bruce's Watson seem like a towering intellect whose skull might well be coveted by a Dr. Mortimer—Dennis Hoey's imbecilic Lestrade—does nothing to stop the slaughter, as the Good Comrades are knocked off one by one. The slapstick Bruce and Hoey both produce (Watson at one point unknowingly dialogues with an owl!) mar the creepy effect screenwriter Roy Chanslor aimed at. There are plot holes, unsurprisingly—as in the canonical Hound, there's no recent history of the curse's efficacy that would naturally be expected—if Alistair's father went whole to his grave, why would anyone take the prophecy seriously? The solution, which I won't spoil here, will surprise some, but some contemporary viewers who have seen variations of it in other contexts, will easily anticipate it. While *The House of Fear* is not one of the best Rathbone/Bruce outings, it comfortably fits in the middle rank.

The Holmes-Ripper film *A Study in Terror* featured a detective frantic to stop the next murder. The tension of that premise, which would also obtain in a Ten Little Indians-like plot, is compelling enough that there's very reason to expect that someone will use it again in a Holmes film. It's recently appeared in print—French author J.M. Erre's *Le Mystere Sherlock*, a 2012 novel not yet translated into English, is set in Meiringen itself. Ten academics have gathered—one of whom will be chosen to head the Sorbonne's new department dedicated to Holmes. After the group is cut off from the outside world by a blizzard, someone begins knocking off the professors, one by one. Erre's approach is somewhat tongue-in-cheek, as in the section where the Christie novel is used as a guide by the survivors to stay alive.

Readers interested in a more serious approach will be delighted to happen upon Locked Room International's latest from Paul Halter, justifiably labeled as John Dickson Carr's heir in crafting clever puzzles, and even cleverer solutions to them. *The Invisible Circle*, set in a castle off the Cornish coast, features a number of impossible crimes, including one committed in a locked room, apparently by a killer wielding Excalibur itself. The tensions mounts to a fever-pitch as the murderer begins stalking everyone trapped in the castle.

The plot structure isn't a natural fit for the Cumberbatch or Downey series, and isn't easily squeezed into the forty-five-minute or so length of an episode of *Elementary*; for now, the latter (whose star, Johnny Lee Miller starred in *Mindhunters*, in which the people being taken out one by one are all FBI profilers), perhaps in a special extended episode or multi-parter, is the best bet for a Holmesian adaptation of the story. In the interim, 2015 will see the BBC three-part adaptation of Christie's original, one that may finally adhere to the grim spirit of the original and faithfully translate it to the screen, even if the power of subtle suggestion is a challenge for any filmmaker.

Lenny Picker, a freelance writer in New York City, who recognizes his hubris in even thinking Christie's solution to her own puzzle missed the mark, can be reached at lpicker613@gmail.com.

ASK MRS HUDSON

by Mrs Martha Hudson

I am ever so grateful to my friend Mrs Amalie Warren for filling in for me with this column. However, I do need to correct one error that she understandably made in reference to my late husband Archibald. She states that he took up residence as a private investigator in the New World, specifically, Manhattan. But she has confused the issue. He did not go there, but rather to some place in the state of Ohio. He had a son with the same name, and it was he who eventually travelled eastward.

And now for a few bits of correspondence.

✗   ✗   ✗   ✗

Dear Mrs Hudson—

I am ever so puzzled how you have been able to tolerate the erratic behaviours of Mr Holmes over the years. I concede that he is, of course, a genius, and violin playing in the middle of the night is not so terrible a thing to deal with, but obnoxiously-odourous chemicals? Ragamuffins and shady characters visitng at all hours? And shooting holes in the walls for target practice—*really*!!

You must possess the patience of a saint.

Miffed in Mulberry

✗   ✗   ✗   ✗

Dear Miffed,

There was a time, I do admit, when I seriously considered asking my tenant to find other lodgings, but there are three reasons why I came to put up with it all. First of all, and I do admit that this displays a certain degree of cupidity on my part, but Mr Holmes and Dr Watson were always prompt with their monthly rent, and I have been a landlady long enough to know that this is not always the case. Secondly, both gentlemen are ever so considerate and caring…well, the good doctor certainly is, and I do think his influence to some extent has mellowed his companion. Finally, when I perceived how Mr Holmes's detectival investigations not only righted injustices, but assuaged the fears and tensions of his clients (especially the women!), I determined to accept his many idiosyncracies as the price for the privilege of having him as my tenant.

I did, however, put a stop to his "bullet-carving" the initials V. R., on my walls!

Yours Truly,
Mrs Hudson

✗   ✗   ✗   ✗

Dear Mrs Hudson,

Do you know what sort of music Mr Holmes liked to play on his violin?

Harmoniously Curious

✗   ✗   ✗   ✗

Dear Harmoniously Curious,

I did have to ask him about this. His musical tastes are wide-ranging, though he is especially fond of Beethoven. However, the one composition I have heard him play more often than any other is Bach's Chaconne in D Minor, which he says is the fifth and final movement of the Partita Number Two.

This is a lengthy piece; it takes him perhaps twenty minutes to play, and it is always the final music of the night. It is—he tells me—in the form of a theme and variations. The theme, I can tell you, is quite haunting.

Yours Truly,
Mrs Hudson

✗   ✗   ✗   ✗

Dear Mrs Hudson,

Have you ever heard Sherlock Holmes tell a joke?
Risible in Rochester

✗   ✗   ✗   ✗

Dear Risible,

Never.
Yours Very Truly,
Mrs Hudson

✗   ✗   ✗   ✗

Dear Mrs Hudson,

Dr Watson assures us that Mr Holmes had no romantic interest whatsoever with Irene Adler, but with all due respect to him, I would sooner trust your woman's instinct. Was the Great Detective ever smitten?

Eager in Edinburgh

✗　✗　✗　✗

Dear Eager,

I am amused that a Scot would show interest in such matters, so I conclude that you are *not* a man, but a woman. Had you asked me this at some earlier time, I certainly would have said *No*, but in this issue Dr Watson has finally convinced Mr Holmes to allow him to tell a secret that I had not known about. I suggest that you read *The Adventure of the Nine Hole League*.

Sincerely Yours,
Mrs Hudson

✗　✗　✗　✗

Dear Mrs Hudson,

How did you learn that Mr Holmes had not died at Reichenbach?

Concerned in Chichester

✗　✗　✗　✗

Dear Concerned,

Dear, dear Dr Watson was ever so kindly about it. Late one afternoon, he surprised me by dropping by—he had not been living at 221 for some time—and invited me to dinner. At the end of the meal, over tea and cake he solicitiously insisted on taking my pulse and temperature, and he even listened to my lungs. Naturally, by this time I was aware that something was "up"! Then, and only after he'd reassured himself of my sturdy good health, did he make his revelation.

I rather surprised him, then, by telling him that in my heart, I was absolutely certain that Mr Holmes was not dead, though I had only my distaff intuition to go by. At that point, Mr Holmes appeared before us, and I am amused to tell you how disconcerted he was when I gave him a huge hug!

Very Truly Yours,
Mrs Hudson

✗　✗　✗　✗

I always like to share recipes with my readers. Here are two, one of which thoroughly mystified both Dr Watson and Mr Holmes. But first, here is a fish dish that delighted my illustrious tenants. It is an Israeli dish that a neighbour introduced me to, and its original-language name is—

DAG BANANA BISHKEDEEM

4 large fillets of sole
2 bananas, halved the long way
½ cup blanched, slivered almonds
3 tablespoons of butter, plus ¼ cup butter
flour
salt and pepper, to taste
2 tablespoons of chopped parsley
½ lemon

Method:

1. Coat fish in flour and season with salt and pepper.
2. Sauté in hot butter for about ten minutes, or till lightly brown on both sides, then remove fish to a warm platter.
3. To skillet used to fry the fish, add ¼ cup of butter and heat. Add the bananas and sauté for two or three minutes till bananas are lightly brown.
4. Place half of a banana on each of the four fish pieces.
5. Into the skillet add ½ cup of almonds and sauté till light brown. Turn off heat.
6. To the almonds, add the juice of ½ lemon and also, 2 tablespoons of the chopped parsley.
7. Mix pan to combine ingredients and pour it over the fish.

When I first served my gentlemen the following dessert, they complimented me on it being "such an excellent apple pie." Well, I astounded them both by stating that I used no apples at all, and then challenged either of them to solve the mystery. That is perhaps the only time that I remember hearing Mr Holmes laugh out loud!

APPLE PIE WITHOUT APPLES

20 whole Saltines or Ritz crackers
1 ¼ cups of sugar
2 teaspoons of cream of tartar
½ teaspoon of cinammon
2 cups of water
1 pie crust, top and bottom

Method:
1. Bring water to a boil without stirring it.
2. Add the crackers and boil for two minutes, again without stirring, then set it aside to cool.
3. Pour on the crust and put chunks of butter on top, then put the top crust on.
4. Bake at 425 degrees for twenty-five minutes.

THE ADVENTURE OF THE SHERLOCK HOLMES CHOCOLATE CARDS

by Gary Lovisi

Following in the footsteps of The Great Detective many of us seek out the more outre aspects of being a Sherlock Holmes fan by collecting unusual items relating to our hero. In doing so, it is possible to find odd items relating to him that are fascinating, often rare, but again always fun. Some of the best of these are the picture cards that were done for an obscure and long-forgotten chocolate maker in Barcelona, Spain, over eight decades ago!

Now there are a lot of Holmes-related picture cards out there. Going way back to the early 20th century there were many Sherlock Holmes cigarette picture cards and series. These were small cards included free inside cigarette packages of the era. There are various sets of these, mostly from the UK, and they are all avidly collected.

However, just as desirable, and even more rare, is the generally unknown series of the "Chocolate Jaime Boix" cards. These are not cigarette cards, but are what are termed "trade cards," printed for business advertising. These cards are larger than cigarette cards, roughly being the size of a standard postal card, and they feature a color illustration from a story of the canon on one side, and text in Spanish about the illustration and story on the other side—along with advertising information that gives the chocolate makers name and address in Barcelona.

These cards are quite simply a lovely group of Sherlock Holmes illustrated images. The cards comprise three series that total 40 cards, none are dated, but they are from the 1930s.

Series A tells the story of "The Musgrave Ritual" ("El Ritual de los Musgrave" from the *Adventures of Sherlock Holmes*), in ten cards, numbered 1 to 10.

Series B recounts "The Speckled Band" ("La Banda Moteada"), with ten cards numbered 11 to 20.

Series C tells the tale of "The Sign of the Four" ("La Marca de los Cuarto"), this time taking 20 cards to illustrate the story, cards numbered 21 to 40.

The first card in each of the three series is a charming title card, featuring the name of the Holmes adventure and a design and illustration that captures some aspect of that particular story. The exception is the Series A #1 card, which is the first card in the set, and acts as a title card for the entire set. It is titled "Aventuras de Sherlock Holmes" and has an excellent image of Holmes with arms crossed, pipe in mouth, looking thoughtful as his eyes gaze over his London domain. Quite impressive. The rest of the cards offer terrific artwork depicting Holmes and Watson, along with various characters and villains from the three stories.

El Ritual de los Musgrave
Série A.—Núm. 8

... un cuerpo humano, encogido...

El Ritual de los Musgrave
Série A.—Núm. 7

Bajamos una escalera...

The art on cards 2, 7, and 8 of "The Musgrave Ritual" offer us stark images of murder as Holmes and Watson find a body while they investigate the Musgrave estate. Card 21, the title card for "The Sign of The Four," shows some of the stolen treasure behind this dark case. Cards 16 and 17 for "The Speckled Band" feature images of Holmes and Watson with an agitated and villainous Dr. Roylott, and in the latter card, with a pensive Miss Stoner.

El Ritual de los Musgrave
Série A.—Núm. 9

Brunton estaba en su poder.

The art on all these cards is quite good, and while the artist is unknown—the art *is* signed but it is difficult to make out the name—it appears to be something like "cell Soliolifoto." The art is reminiscent of that seen on the covers of dime novels of the early 20th century, a bit more formal than we are used to today, but it offers a view into a past world that now is long gone. Regardless, the images are bright and colorful, accurate to the canon and full of suspense and wonder—which is just the way we love to see our Sherlock Holmes and his Watson.

Aventuras de Sherlock Holmes
Série B.—Núm. 11

These cards are incredibly rare, and a set of all 40 cards is virtually impossible to obtain and would likely cost hundreds of dollars. The individual cards sell from $10 to $25 depending on condition and the image on the card—obviously cards depicting Holmes and Watson go for a higher price.

La Banda Moteada
Série B.—Núm. 16

Y cogiendo las tenazas de la chimenea...

Aventuras de Sherlock Holmes
Série C.—Núm. 31

LA MARCA DE LOS CUATRO

Colección de 48 dibujos

As if this series isn't impossible enough to complete, full disclosure forces me to at least mention that there is an even earlier and even more rare series of Spanish chocolate trade cards from the 1920s: the "El Detective Sherlock Holmes" ten card series put out by Fabrica de Chocolate de Jaime Torras Arano—but we'll leave this one as fodder for another article, on another day.

To sum up, the 1930s Spanish Chocolate Jaime Boix trade card series offers 40 wonderful visions from three classic Holmes stories that surely will stimulate any Sherlockian collector's appetite for the rare and obscure relating to The Great Detective. These unusual cards are great fun to collect, but it can be frustrating because they are nearly impossible to find—which is why it is such an adventure to locate them and complete a set—but they are well worth your search. As Holmes himself might tell us, half the fun is in the hunt. So let the adventure begin!

[I would like to thank Robert C. Hess for his kind assistance with information for this article.]

GARY LOVISI is a Sherlock Holmes fan, collector and pastiche author whose story "The Adventure of The Missing Detective" was nominated by the Mystery Writers of America for a Best Short Story Edgar Award. Lovisi has also written various stories and articles in *Sherlock Holmes Mystery Magazine*, as well as the book *Sherlock Holmes: The Great Detective in Paperback & Pastiche* (Gryphon Books, 2008). His latest book is *The Great Detective: His Further Adentures* (Borgo Press, 2012), an anthology he edited of Holmes pastiches. You can find out more about him and his work at his website: *www.gryphonbooks.com*

SHERLOCK HOLMES ÍNTIMO

Sherlock Holmes, hombre pulido y correcto en el vestir y en la conversación, era, en cambio, muy desordenado en su vida íntima. No era raro verle sacar el tabaco de una zapatilla, sujetar las cartas por contestar con un cuchillo sobre la puerta, ó dibujar á balazos iniciales en la pared, para ejercitarse, cómodamente sentado, á tirar al blanco.

Nuestro cuarto estaba atestado de chirimbolos de química, piezas de convicción, etc., colocado lo mismo sobre una silla que en el tarro de la manteca. Pero ¡los papeles!, que lo cubrían todo, eran lo que más molestaba. Holmes no rompía ningún documento, ningún periódico, ninguna carta. No obstante, cada dos años, hacía un esfuerzo para poner los papeles en orden, dudando mucho antes de romper algo.

Sherlock Holmes era inconsecuente por temperamento. Tan pronto desplegaba gran energía y actividad, como dejábase caer sobre un sofá, horas tras horas, días tras días, con un libro en la mano, adormeciéndose con las melodías de un violín. Durante estos períodos, hasta costábale trabajo arrastrarse hacia la mesa para comer. Así se comprende que los papeles fueran ganando el cuarto y los muebles y hasta nosotros mismos.

Colección de 40 dibujos

REGALO Á LOS CONSUMIDORES

DEL

Chocolate Jaime Boix

HOSPITAL, 46—BARCELONA

J. Horta, impresor, Méndez Núñez

A MOST VALUABLE INSTITUTION

How Sherlock Holmes Used the Press

by Dan Andriacco

"The Press, Watson, is a most valuable institution, if only you know how to use it."

When Sherlock Holmes says that, in "The Adventure of the Six Napoleons," he isn't just delivering a throw-away line for effect. He is revealing one of the secrets of his success as a sleuth. Throughout his career, Holmes effectively uses the Press in a number of different ways.

In "The Six Napoleons," Holmes has Lestrade tell the journalist Horace Harker "that I have quite made up my mind, and that it is certain that a dangerous homicidal maniac, with Napoleonic delusions, was in his house last night." The hapless Harker publishes this bunk, which achieves Holmes's aim of lulling the killer and thief Beppo into a false sense of security.

Holmes does something similar in "The Adventure of the Illustrious Client." Having been the victim of a murderous assault, he wants the villain behind the attacks—the infamous Baron Gruner—to believe that he has achieved his goal. "The first thing is to exaggerate my injuries," Holmes tells Watson. "They'll come to you for news. Put it on thick, Watson. Lucky if I live the week out—concussion—delirium—what you like! You can't overdo it." Watson does his job: "For six days the public were under the impression that Holmes was at the door of death."

These instances of Holmes using the Press for *dis*information are rare. Most often he uses the newspapers, and sometimes journalists, for *in*formation. Holmes is an omnivorous reader of the papers, clipping and pasting into his "good old index" ads and articles of astonishing variety. Equally amazing is his filing system. Thus we find in the V volume: the voyage of the Gloria Scott; Victor Lynch, the forger; venomous lizard or gila; Vittoria, the circus belle; Vanderbilt and the Yeggman; vipers; Vigor, the Hammersmith wonder; vampirism in Hungary and vampirism in Transylvania (SUSS).

Holmes seems to have regarded "the agony columns"—what we now call classified ads—and news stories as equally file-worthy. Nowhere is this clearer than in a passage from "The Adventure of the Red Circle," where Watson writes:

He took down the great book in which, day by day, he filed the agony columns of the various London journals. "Dear me," said he, turning over the pages, "what a chorus of groans, cries, and bleatings! A rag-bag of singular happenings! But surely the most valuable hunting ground that was ever given to a student of the unusual."

And so it was. On this particular occasion, Holmes finds a string of ads in *The Daily Gazette* from one "G," who turns out to be Gennaro Lucca, communicating with his wife, Emilia.

But just think of the many other ads that appear in the Canon, not all of which wound up in the index: Jabez Wilson's helpful assistant points out to him an ad about a tremendous opportunity called the Red-Headed League (REDH). Poor, deluded Mary Sutherland advertises for the missing Hosmer Angel, little dreaming how lost that cause was (CASE). An ad for a missing engineer causes Holmes to comment with dark humor, "Ha! That represents the last time the colonel needed to have his machine overhauled, I fancy" (ENGI). Violet Hunter both advertises and answers ads when looking for a position as a governess (COPP). Mycroft Holmes, that least energetic of men, stirs himself to place an ad "in all the dailies" offering a reward for information about Paul Kratides from Athens and "a Greek lady whose first name is Sophy" (GREE). It is "an advertisement in the *Times*" that lures music teacher Violet Smith into such a perilous position in the home of Mr. Carruthers (SOLI). The spy Hugo Oberstein communicates with Colonel Valentine Walter through ads in *The Daily Telegraph*, which Holmes uses to his advantage by taking out an ad of his own under Oberstein's pseudonym to trap Walter.

Sherlock Holmes himself also places ads, although not as often as you might think. I count five times, from key actions in *A Study in Scarlet* and *The Sign of Four* to an ad that finds no takers in

"The Naval Treaty," to a passing mention in "The Disappearance of Lady Frances Carfax." Most memorable for me is the scene in "The Adventure of the Blue Carbuncle" where Holmes writes: "Found at the corner of Goodge Street, a goose and a black felt hat. Mr. Henry Baker can have the same by applying at 6:30 this evening at 221B Baker Street." He then tells Peterson, the commissionaire, to "run down to the advertising agency and have this put in the evening papers."

"In which, sir?"

"Oh, in the *Globe, Star, Pall Mall, St. James's, Evening News Standard, Echo*, and any others that occur to you."

"And any others that occur to you?" Just the mention of six evening newspapers in one city, even in the capital city of the British Empire at its height, is enough to make anyone acquainted with the sad state of 21st century newspapers weep. Other Holmes stories refer to whole crop of additional London dailies: *The Standard* (STUD), *The Chronicle* (REDH, CARD), *The Daily Gazette* (REDC), *The Morning Post* (NOBL), *The Daily Telegraph* (STUD, COPP, BRUC), *The Daily News* (STUD, GREE), and of course *The Times* (SIGN, HOUN).

Holmes consults back issues of *The Times* in *The Sign of Four*, proving that the good old index doesn't have everything. Indeed, although Sherlock Holmes was a tireless reader and clipper of newspapers, it seems that some items of note do get past him. Yes, he knows about the Countess of Morcar's stolen blue carbuncle from reading the advertisement in *The Times* every day. But he somehow misses the account of what Watson calls "the vanishing of the lady" in "The Adventure of the Noble Bachelor," even though it was written up in *The Morning Post* and he has all the newspapers on his stack. Nor does he recall reading about the death of Arthur Cadogan West in "The Adventure of the Bruce-Partington Plans," although Watson remembers and manages to find the account "among the litter of papers upon the sofa."

Even when Holmes is generally aware of a case, though, he often turns to the newspapers to acquire more in-depth knowledge. For example, as he and Watson hurdle toward Exeter at fifty-three and a half miles an hour, the detective dips into "the bundle of fresh papers which he procured at Paddington" to get the latest news on the murder of John Straker and the disappearance of Silver Blaze. I think we can assume that Holmes never entirely trusts the accuracy of such accounts. Nevertheless, he often uses them as a starting point.

So familiar is Holmes with the daily Press that he can distinguish their type faces, although he humbly confesses to Watson in *The Hound of the Baskervilles* that "once when I was very young I confused the *Leeds Mercury* with *The Western Morning News*."

Unlike Nero Wolfe, who frequently calls on the inside knowledge of a journalist named Lon Cohen, Sherlock Holmes has no long-term relationship with a member of the Press. In the later years of his career, however, he forms a bond with an unusual character named Langdale Pike. As Watson tells it:

Langdale Pike was his human book of reference upon all matters of social scandal. This strange, languid creature spent his waking hours in the bow window of a St. James's Street club and was the receiving-station as well as the transmitter for all the gossip of the metropolis. He made, it was said, a four-figure income by the paragraphs which he contributed every week to the garbage papers which cater to an inquisitive public…Holmes helped Langdale to knowledge, and on occasion was helped in turn. (3GAB)

The only other journalists Holmes encounters are Neville St. Clair, otherwise known as "The Man with the Twisted Lip," and Isadora Persano, "the well-known journalist and duelist, who was found stark staring mad with a match box in front of him which contained a remarkable worm said to be unknown to science" (THOR). For full details on the Persano case, consult Watson's tin dispatch box.

Despite his apparent inattention to cultivating the Press, Holmes's cases frequently are well reported long before Dr. Watson takes up his pen. In fact, that is the very reason that some of the cases don't make their way into the Canon. At the beginning of "The Five Orange Pips," in explaining why he had chosen not to record certain adventures, the good doctor notes that "Some, however, have already gained publicity through the newspapers…" (FIVE)

Shockingly, as noted earlier, Press accounts in *those* days were not always fully accurate. A newspaper called *The Echo* wraps up the murders of Enoch Drebber and Joseph Stangerson by noting:

It is an open secret that the credit of this smart capture belongs entirely to the well-known Scotland Yard officials, Messrs. Lestrade and Gregson. The man was apprehended, it appears, in the rooms of a certain Mr. Sherlock Holmes, who has himself, as an amateur, shown some talent in the detective line and who, with such instructors, may hope in time to attain some degree of their skill. (STUD)

That prompted Watson to write *A Study in Scarlet* to set the record straight.

The twists and turns of the Sholto affair are covered in *The Standard* and other papers, starting with a story headed "Mysterious Business at Upper Norwood," which mentions Holmes and Watson on its way to praising Athelney Jones. The false arrest of Thaddeus Sholto and the rest of the household does nothing to shake the newspaper's faith in Jones. After reporting the release of Thaddeus and the housekeeper, *The Standard* confidently adds: "It is believed, however, that the police have a clue as to the real culprits, and that it is being prosecuted by Mr. Athelney Jones, of Scotland Yard, with all his well-known energy and sagacity. Further arrests may be expected at any moment." (SIGN)

In the very late "Adventure of the Retired Colourman," this situation seems to have changed hardly at all. The bi-weekly *North Surrey Observer* gives full credit to Inspector McKinnon for solving the case. "Brilliant Police Investigation," says the subhead on the story. It is quoted at length on the very last page of the Doubleday *Complete Sherlock Holmes*.

It appears, though, that as the years go on the newspapers in general treat Holmes more favorably. At the time of "The Final Problem," the married Watson seems to have been following Holmes's career largely through the Press. He writes in the opening paragraphs: "During the winter of that year [1890] and the spring of 1891, I saw in the papers that he had been engaged by the French government upon a matter of supreme importance..."

Even traveling in disguise and under a false name Holmes is good copy. After his dramatic return from the dead, he tells Watson in "The Adventure of the Empty House": "You may have read of the remarkable explorations of a Norwegian named Sigerson, but I am sure that it never occurred to you that you were receiving news of your friend."

Like anyone who deals with the Press, Holmes knows that the only way to ensure complete accuracy is to write it himself. This he does early in his acquaintance with Dr. Watson, penning an article called "The Book of Life." "From a drop of water," he writes, "a logician could infer the possibility of an Atlantic or a Niagara without having seen or heard of one or the other." Not knowing that his new roommate was the author, Dr. Watson's reaction upon reading this is unambiguous: "What ineffable twaddle! I never read such rubbish in my life" (SCAN).

Aside from his monographs, Holmes as writer is best known as the author of two of his own later adventures, "The Adventure of the Blanched Soldier" and "The Adventure of the Lion's Mane." In addition to these stories, he is almost certainly the author of two long letters to the editors of daily newspapers in which he attempts to solve puzzling crimes from his armchair. These are recorded in two short stories by Arthur Conan Doyle, published as part of his *Round the Fire* series in *The Strand* magazine in 1898 while Holmes was believed dead.

In "The Man with the Watches," we read: "There was a letter in the *Daily Gazette*, over the signature of a well-known criminal investigator, which gave rise to considerable discussion at the time. He had formed a hypothesis which had at least ingenuity to recommend it…" The strict logical framework of that letter, written in 1892, leaves little doubt as to identity of the "well-known criminal investigator" in question.

And there can be no doubt at all as to the author of a letter to *The Times* of London on July 3, 1890, as reported in "The Lost Special." The letter starts out with this tell-tale introduction: "It is one of the elementary principles of practical reasoning that when the impossible has been eliminated, the residuum, however improbable, must contain the truth."

In addition to clearly having the same author, these two letters have one other thing in common: They both set forth theories that are flat-out wrong. I think, therefore, that the reason Arthur Conan Doyle recorded these cases rather than Dr. Watson is quite…elementary.

From this survey of the Canon and beyond, we have numerous concrete examples of why Holmes found the Press a most valuable institution. He used it for information, for disinformation, as a tool for finding people and things, and as a medium for broadcasting his ideas. Although in the early years the newspapers slighted his achievements in favor of the official police, that changed—for the most part—as he built his reputation...with the help of Dr. Watson.

Watson must have been almost as well acquainted with the newspapers as his some-time roommate. For one thing, he often reads Press accounts out loud to Holmes, causing at least one scholar to question whether Holmes was illiterate. Most importantly, in at least thirteen stores—from *A Study in Scarlet* through "The Adventure of Wisteria Lodge"—Watson the writer tells the story in part by quoting a large chunk of copy from one or more newspaper accounts of the case. Perhaps Holmes was preaching to the choir when he lectured Watson about the value of the Press...if only you know how to use it.

✗

LIVING THE LIE

by Marc Bilgrey

"Will you miss me, Dave?" said Sally, as she looked out the passenger side window of the light blue Packard.

Dave held the steering wheel tightly and kept his eyes on the road. For a minute he forgot his name. Since he'd only had it for six months, it was an easy mistake to make. He kept telling himself it was Dave, like *Davy Crockett*, the hottest program on television.

"Sure I'll miss you," said Dave, staring at a police car in the rearview mirror. His heart began beating faster. He watched the patrol car drive up behind him, then silently turn onto a side street and disappear. Dave let out a deep breath, glanced at Sally sitting next to him, then at a passing sign that read Train Station, ¼ Mile.

"It'll be the first time we've been separated," she said.

"Oh, come on, it'll only be for a week. You make it sound like you're going on a trip around the world."

"That's what going back home feels like to me. And now with Mom being sick…" Her voice trailed off.

"She'll probably outlive us all." The train station came into view. Dave glanced at the imposing, dirty, stone building, then slowed the car down as he navigated between taxis.

"You won't forget to feed Scooter, will you?"

"How many times do we have to go over this? I'll stop by your place every night and feed the cat, don't worry."

"Okay," said Sally, as they pulled up in front of a cab which was disgorging a group of tourists.

Dave got out, opened the trunk, pulled out Sally's suitcase and placed it on the sidewalk. Sally put her arms around Dave and kissed him.

"I'm gonna miss you so much," she said.

Dave looked into her sparkling green eyes and said, "Just don't be talking to any of those Midwest guys."

"Oh," she said, playfully slapping him on the arm, "you're impossible."

Dave kissed her cheek and said, "Me and Scooter'll be counting the days."

She smiled, picked up her suitcase, turned around and walked into the station.

On the drive back, Dave turned on the radio. The Platters sang, *You've Got That Magic Touch.* Dave thought about Sally. It occurred to him that he really would miss her. He was already starting to feel lonely. The feeling surprised him. He'd vowed to himself when they'd met that he wouldn't get too involved. She was there to pass the time with, to have some fun with, interchangeable with a hundred other women. Though he had tried to maintain his emotional distance, he had realized early on that it was a losing battle.

A police car with flashing lights appeared behind him. Dave felt his throat go dry as he gripped the steering wheel so hard his knuckles turned white. The police car passed him and then zoomed down the highway. Dave swallowed and relaxed his hold on the wheel.

If it hadn't been for Sally, he'd probably have left a month or two earlier. He knew he was pressing his luck. They hadn't called him Doc for no reason. He'd been the brains, the logical one who thought things out. There was no place for emotion, he'd told them. And yet, here he was, ignoring his own advice.

Dave slowed the car down as he passed a movie theater. There was a new Bob Hope picture playing. It looked good, but he decided he just wasn't in the mood. He considered going back to his apartment. What was the point of that? Just to sit and stare at the four walls or watch his new television set? Besides, at this hour, all that was on was *Howdy Doody* or *The Lone Ranger*. He pulled up to a bar and found a parking space.

Inside the bar it was dark and reeked of stale cigarette smoke. He found an empty stool and sat down. An old man at the far end of the bar nursed a drink. The bartender asked Dave what he wanted. He ordered a beer and then chewed on a couple of pretzels from a bowl next to him. The jukebox was playing Doris Day singing *"Que Sera Sera."*

The bartender brought his drink, collected on it and then went to the other side of the counter. Dave took a sip of beer and looked at his reflection in the mirror behind the bar. He had dark circles under his eyes. And no matter how many times he saw his mustache and beard he couldn't get used to them. He'd stopped shaving the day after he'd begun his new life. And even so, there'd been a few close calls.

In Boston a year earlier, a man in a hotel lobby had called him by his old name. They'd gone to high school together. "You must be mistaking me for someone else," said Dave. He left Boston that night. It was probably just an innocent, accidental meeting, but why take chances?

One time, when he was living in Chicago, a newspaper ran an article on the case and printed his picture. He was out of town before the afternoon edition. That's why it was so odd to stay where he was. He'd taken to moving even when there were no incidents. He took another sip of his drink and watched the bartender ring up a sale on the cash register. His thoughts drifted back to *that* day a year and a half earlier. The armored car, the bundles of neatly wrapped new hundred dollar bills. "See you guys back at the warehouse," he'd said. Then he'd gotten into his car and driven away. He wondered how long it had taken them to realize that he wasn't coming back. A day? A week?

"This seat taken?" said a voice.

Dave snapped out of his daze and look to his left as a burly man in a rumpled suit and tie sat down next to him. Dave shrugged.

"Bartender," said the man, "I'll have a glass of your best whiskey." Then the man turned to Dave and said, "When I say life insurance, what comes into your mind?"

Dave got up, placed a quarter on the bar and headed toward the door.

"Hey," said the man, "you don't have to be downright rude."

Dave walked out of the bar and back to his car. A minute later he was driving through the streets. He stopped at a red light and forgot where he was. He was used to it. After a while, every place started looking the same. The greasy spoons, the gas stations, the drive-ins.

He hadn't realized that it would be like this. When he'd taken the money he'd thought that he'd be able to retire and just lie by a pool somewhere, surrounded by palm trees and nubile young women in bathing suits, but it hadn't worked out that way. A few days after he'd left, he'd gone to Florida, rented a house, bought a sports car, a boat, new clothes. A couple of weeks later, he noticed that one of the local cops seemed to always be driving around his house. That was when he realized that he'd never be able to sit in a chaise longue with a cold drink in his hand and watch the world go by. Oh, the money was safe. He'd buried it in a secret place, that wasn't a problem, not for Doc. Nor was coming up with fake I.D. and a new life history. That wasn't a problem, either. What *was* a problem was always having to look over his shoulder.

Even Sally had noticed it. He'd told her that he was neurotic. Phobic was more like it. A fear of cops or feds, or anybody in a uniform, or in a suit and tie, who looked a little too serious.

But what he was really worried about was the old gang. After what he'd done, he knew they'd never stop looking for him. When he hadn't returned to the warehouse that night, it was no longer about just the money. He'd even thought about giving the money back, but he knew it wouldn't solve anything. They'd still hunt him down. At least with it, he had a fighting chance.

Dave stopped the car in front of a boarded-up nightclub and walked across the street to a small park. He sat down on a bench under a shady tree. A couple of teenagers in leather jackets went by. A woman wheeling a baby carriage strolled past, followed by a young couple holding hands.

Dave thought about Sally again. He'd met her six months earlier at the diner where she worked. He thought she looked beautiful in her white waitress uniform. He started going back to the restaurant just to see her. Eventually he asked her out. She'd believed his story about being a financial consultant. At first Dave thought it was just a fling, a casual liaison in a strange town. Then, as the months went by, he actually wondered if he should tell her the truth. Finally, he decided that the best thing for both of them was to live the lie.

But he couldn't deny he had feelings for her that went beyond the physical. "Doc don't feel, he just thinks," was what one of the guys used to say. And for the most part it was true.

"Bang bang!" yelled a child.

Dave turned and saw two little boys wearing coonskin caps, and pointing toy muskets at each other. He got up and walked back to the car.

A few minutes later, he pulled into the parking lot of a super-market and got out. *Now what the hell was it that Scooter eats?* he thought, as he walked into the store.

He found the cat food section and stared at the different brands. They all had colorful labels and cute names. Then he remembered that Sally had mentioned that she had stocked up on cat food before she'd left. What was he doing here? He shrugged. Maybe Scooter would want some kind of special treat. If Sally were Scooter's mother, then he was an uncle, and wasn't that what uncles were for, to spoil kids?

Scooter was a shaded gold Persian that Sally had gotten as a kitten seven years earlier. She'd seen an ad in the newspaper about him. Scooter was the runt of the litter of purebred show cats. Scooter had been real sick and there was some kind of question about whether or not he'd live. Sally had taken him in and nursed him back to health.

Dave would often watch the cat and study his behavior. Dave noticed a lot of things about Scooter. Like how right before it rained, Scooter would start jumping around and scratch the walls and stand up on his hind legs. Then, as soon as it did rain, he'd calm right down. Sometimes Dave would watch how Scooter would sneak up on a spider and then pounce on it and hold the insect under his paw.

And Scooter was always happy to see him. Whenever he'd visit, Scooter would run over and rub up against his leg. Until he'd met Scooter, he hadn't really liked cats, but Scooter was different. Scooter was a real friend. And he wasn't that way with everyone. If Sally had someone over to fix the sink or a squeaky door, Scooter would run and hide.

Dave picked up a few cans, went to the cash register and paid for them. Then he got back into his car and drove out of the parking lot.

On the way to Sally's house, he stopped the car by the bay, got out and watched the sailboats go by. He wondered if the people on them were happy. He took off his jacket and glanced at the sun. Even though it was going down, it was still as warm as it had been earlier in the day. Dave adjusted the gun in the small of his back. On hot days it felt heavier than usual. He looked at the water in the bay and thought about tossing the weapon into it. It was something that had occurred to him many times before. He gave up the idea as he saw a police launch cruise past him. Then he turned around and got back into his car.

A few minutes later, he pulled up to Sally's house. She lived in a residential neighborhood on a quiet, tree-lined street. Dave walked up the path to the house, put the key into the lock, and opened the door.

"Hey, Scooter, Dave's here!" he said, stepping inside and closing the door. No response. "I've got treats for you," he said, shaking the bag of groceries. Still nothing. Dave looked around the living room and saw Scooter under one of the chairs. Scooter tensed up. Dave stood silently. He listened, but didn't hear anything. Then he placed the bag on the floor and pulled out his gun.

As soon as he did he heard a floorboard creak in another room. His heart began pounding. He turned and noticed that one of the windows was open. He took a breath, then tiptoed to the sofa and crouched behind it. He said in a loud voice, "So, how you been Scooter? Good kitty, I've got some food for you."

Just then, a shadow appeared on the wall. It came from the direction of the bedroom. Dave kept talking. "Good boy. I know you like tuna."

A man wearing a dark coat and hat and holding a gun peered out from behind a wall. Then he stepped into the living room. Dave squeezed the trigger of his gun. There was a flash of light and a loud cracking sound as the man moaned, grabbed his stomach and fell to the floor.

Immediately another man with a gun appeared. Dave shot him twice in the chest. He dropped to the carpet and stopped moving. Seconds went by. No one else walked out. Dave looked in the bedroom and then the kitchen, but they were empty. He went back into the living room and stared at the two men. One he recognized. He was the cousin of one of the guys in the gang.

Scooter came over and rubbed up against Dave's leg. Dave let out a breath and said, "You saved my life, boy, you know that?"

Scooter mewed.

"C'mon, Scooter, we have to get out of here."

He grabbed Scooter, got Sally's cat carrier out of the closet, and put Scooter inside. Holding the carrier, Dave cautiously walked outside and back to his car. He stuck Scooter's carrier on the seat next to him and turned on the car's ignition.

Five minutes later, Dave was on the highway heading north. *How had they found him?* he wondered. He must have done something careless. He'd stayed too long in one place, he'd been spotted by someone, he'd—Sally. Sally. She had just coincidentally gone to visit her poor sick mother in Cleveland. Sally. He'd trusted her. Somehow they'd found him and had bought Sally off, or scared her, and she'd cooperated. Could she have known about what they'd intended to do? Maybe they'd told her they were federal agents, something like that. Anyway, she'd gone along and...Dave noticed Scooter looking out of the window of the cat carrier.

Scooter's eyes were big, like he was scared, but he wasn't mewing. Dave glanced back at the road, then at Scooter again as he saw him pushing his paws through the slats in the carrier *It was as if Scooter was in his own little prison*, thought Dave, *a travelling prison.* Dave pressed down on the gas pedal. He wondered where the road would take him and what the next town would be like. Then he realized that it didn't matter. Even though it all seemed like wide open country, everywhere he looked there were locks and guards and iron bars.

A COLD PLACE TO DIE

by J. P. Seewald

"Why must you continue to torture me?"

"Stop moaning and groaning," Barbara said.

Charles Sinclair stared at the gleaming, metal machines that seemed to smile with sadistic delight, enjoying his agony.

Barbara shook her head at him. "You're getting worse and worse." She gripped his arm in a vise-like grip. "Working out at a gym is good for you. You're getting soft and flabby." To emphasize her words, Barbara took a hard swipe at his midsection.

Charles winced. God, she was fast, got him before he even had time to gird himself for the blow.

"Last time you convinced me to come with you, I was sore for a week."

Barbara pursed her lips. "No pain, no gain. Anyway, you just proved my point. It's because you don't come often enough that you have such a paunch."

"Look, you can come here as often as you want, but I don't like it. Why can't we just go for a walk together instead?"

Barbara tossed her mane of tawny hair and frowned at him. "Jogging's all right, but you walk too slowly. And you should exercise everyday."

Charles snorted, "Yeah, right."

"I'm only trying to help you, Charles. I don't want to see you keel over from a heart attack. It could happen you know. You really don't take proper care of yourself." She gave him a pitying look, as if he were some inferior creature. "I'm doing all I can, but you continue to resist."

Good Lord, not another lecture! He hated it when she got into nagging mode, all pompous and superior.

"I don't like this place," he said through gritted teeth. "As far as I'm concerned it's a torture chamber."

Barbara sighed dramatically. "This is a first-rate gym. If you spent half as much time working out as you do complaining, you'd be in top shape by now. Why do you resist me on this when I'm doing it for your own good? I don't expect you to turn into an Adonis overnight, but we could certainly do something about that gut."

Charles caved in, saying, "All right, what do you want me to do here?" She was one tough negotiator.

"Well, since you said you wanted to walk, let's start you off on the treadmill."

It was boring, and he'd much rather be outdoors, walking in the park, but she'd worn him down. As he began working out on the treadmill, Charles thought about the intricacies of his relationship with Barbara.

From the beginning, she'd done the pursuing. He'd just made partner at Guzman, Garfield, Mackenzie, Barker and Lowe. Everyone was congratulating him. Barbara, an up-and-coming associate, had been particularly warm and friendly. When he came back from lunch, he'd found a red rose placed on his desk with a message: "May your success be as fragrant as this flower." She'd signed her name with a flourish.

Several times she came to his office during the next few mornings and asked him some work-related question about a brief or file, nothing she couldn't have really taken care of herself.

Barbara was like a force of nature. She was full of vitality and energy, and she was a passionate lover. He'd never known anyone quite like her. Even at the office, the more Barbara did, the more she seemed capable of doing. Charles had to admire her. He actually envied her ambition and determination. Had he ever been as eager to get ahead as she was? He doubted it.

Marrying Barbara seemed preordained. For a while, they were happy together. But after a few years, it was becoming clear they wanted different things. Charles had grown tired of working twelve hour days, six, sometimes seven days a week. He was pushing forty and getting bored practicing corporate law. He had a respectable investment portfolio, a nice condo, but no real interests beyond his career. He was restless and wanted something more out of life.

Barbara wanted something more as well. Ambition and drive were a part of her very being. She was eager to rise to a position of power in the firm.

Charles watched her working out, glistening with perspiration. Stepping down from an elliptical machine, she slowly walked toward him, toweling off.

"Is that all you've done so far, just the treadmill?"

Twenty minutes had passed, and Charles hadn't taken the machine beyond its second level setting. He didn't bother to answer, knowing instinctively that any excuse would just add fuel to her fire.

"When are you going to let Josh work with you? He's the best personal trainer in the city."

"Anything you approve of is the best," he observed.

"When did you get to be so cynical?"

He shrugged, not eager for a confrontation.

"Josh could probably fit you in today as a favor to me."

"Next time maybe. I'm ready to leave," he said, annoyance slipping from his tongue.

"I'm taking a shower first. What about you?"

"Later, when I get home."

She gave him a look of disappointment, then turned and took off toward the locker rooms. He probably wouldn't need that shower after all. She wasn't about to have sex with him tonight. Charles wasn't certain he really cared any more.

At one time, he found Barbara mysterious. Even after he'd gotten to know her in the biblical sense, he'd never quite comprehended her essence or the demons that drove her. She never talked about her past, her family, even her schooling. But he had learned that what made her tick was the idea of getting ahead. For Barbara, success was an aphrodisiac. It was the only thing that really mattered to her.

The next morning, Charles approached Guzman's secretary, determination etched on his face. "Alice, I need to see the boss."

"Today? He's really busy. Has clients all day."

"It'll just be for a minute. I promise." He gave Alice his friendliest smile.

She'd always had a soft spot for him. She was a shy, pleasant woman but also a capable, competent legal assistant. If he had dated anyone from the firm, it should have been her. But neither of them would ever have approached the other. Well, it was too late now. Regrets stuck in his throat like a fishbone.

Alice gave a shy smile and got him the time he needed with Guzman.

"So what's so important that it can't wait?" his boss looked up, one bushy brow cocked inquiringly.

"I've been thinking that I want a change of pace. Wondered how you'd feel if I looked into practicing criminal law."

Guzman stared at Charles as though he'd just confessed to being an axe murderer. "You know as well as I do all our clients are corporate. That's what we do here, and it's where the money is. Are you thinking of leaving us? Has someone made you an offer?"

"Nothing like that. I just thought I might take on some white collar criminals. Maybe start a new department here at the firm."

"I suppose we could discreetly let certain clients become aware that such services have become available," Guzman conceded. "I don't want to lose you. You're the best in bankruptcy." He frowned. "What does Barbara think about this?"

"I haven't discussed it with her yet."

"Well, if you don't mind advice from an older, more experienced man, I'd talk it over with her before you go any further with the plan." Guzman glanced meaningfully at his gold Rolex. Charles thanked his boss for his time and advice before leaving the office.

He thanked Alice, who gave him another beatific smile, and returned to his own office feeling better, as though he'd undergone some sort of a catharsis.

In spite of Guzman's well-meaning advice, he wasn't eager to discuss his decision with Barbara. It would likely only lead to another quarrel, something he preferred to avoid.

He had too much of family feuding in his childhood. By the time his parents finally decided to divorce, he'd actually felt relieved. He couldn't stand the constant turmoil. He craved a peaceful environment. Maybe he just wasn't cut out for marriage. He'd let Barbara push him into a relationship that wasn't right for either of them. It was becoming painfully apparent that they weren't suited. The marriage was becoming torture.

A few weeks later, both he and Barbara were summoned to Guzman's office. Guzman, not one to waste a moment of his valuable, billable time, got right to the point. "I have a client who I think you both might want to work with. You're aware that Williams Industries is one of our corporate clients. Well, Vance Williams has some problems."

"Vance Williams, the eccentric heir to millions?" Barbara asked.

"More like billions," Guzman said with a wry smile.

"Is his company moving into bankruptcy?" Barbara's eyes were dewy with avid interest.

"Not exactly." Guzman cleared his throat. "Williams does have some tax issues that he'll need your help with, Barbara. But he also has another kind of problem. His wife disappeared."

"I read something about that in the newspaper," Charles said.

"I told Williams you might be able to help him, Charles. It seems the police have been sniffing around."

Barbara looked bewildered. "Why would Charles be able to help?"

Guzman turned to him. "You didn't tell her, did you?"

"Tell me what?" Barbara asked.

Charles pulled at his collar and loosened his tie which was feeling like a noose. "I'm looking to take on some criminal work."

Barbara took it better than he'd expected, or maybe that was just for Guzman's benefit. She could be a consummate actress when she chose.

"Williams will be sending a car to pick you up at two o'clock."

Charles stared at Guzman. "He's not coming to the office?"

"He rarely leaves that compound of his. Williams is a recluse."

As far as Charles was concerned, Williams was just a lunatic who'd inherited a lot of money, but he kept his opinion to himself. "How can Williams run a major company from his house?"

"He can and does."

"He must have been in to see you," Charles said to Guzman.

"I've mostly dealt with his executives—although he'll phone personally when he wants something important done, like he did today. Anyway, this is a real opportunity if you want to practice criminal law. You'll be starting with a big name client."

"That's assuming there is a case."

"He sounded edgy on the phone." Guzman tapped his pen thoughtfully.

"Imagine meeting an actual billionaire and working for him," Barbara said.

That pretty much settled the matter. Arguing with Barbara against the meeting would have been as sensible as standing outdoors during a twister, and not nearly as pleasant.

They were picked up in style by a foreign-looking driver with black, slicked-back hair driving a black limo. Both the car and driver looked sinister to Charles. Williams's chauffeur reminded him of a thug.

Williams's estate was situated on eighteen acres of prime countryside and provided considerable privacy. A rough-looking character answered the door, someone who looked a lot more like a bouncer or a bodyguard than a butler. The billionaire kept them waiting for quite a while.

Williams finally entered the large living room. The man was easily in his middle fifties, looking fit and tan, and dressed casually in a knit shirt, jeans, and joggers. The clothing looked to be of the best quality. He definitely did not appear to be a wild eccentric or a doddering recluse. Although Charles had represented some very wealthy, successful people, he'd never before met a billionaire and wasn't certain what to expect.

They introduced themselves. Barbara was back to being the charming woman he'd married—and then some. The meal they were served in the cavernous dining room might have been good, but it tasted like sawdust to him because Barbara was busy flirting with Williams right there in front of him. Williams and Barbara did most of the talking.

After dinner, they discussed legal matters. Barbara took the tax information.

"I'll get back to you as soon as I've crunched some numbers," she promised in a purring voice.

"Smart and pretty. You're a very lucky man," Williams said.

"Let's talk about your wife's disappearance."

"Police detectives came by. Acted like they thought I had something to do with it."

"And did you?"

Williams's smile didn't quite reach his eyes. "Are you on my side? If I'm going to retain you, that's something I have to know."

"I just need to get the facts straight. Did you report your wife missing?"

"No, that would be my wife's sister."

"How long was she gone?"

"About a month."

Charles was surprised. "And you didn't think to report it?"

Williams shook his head. "We had an argument. She drove off. Said she was leaving me."

"If the police get in touch with you again, tell them you won't speak without an attorney present. There's an old saying that a fish can't be hooked unless it opens its mouth."

"Won't they think I'm hiding something?"

"They already do. Call me immediately if they contact you again."

Williams insisted on giving them a tour of the mansion before they left. Barbara was eager; she looped her hands like tentacles around the rich man's arm. Williams led them upstairs first. The marble foyer had a grand staircase that divided to two different wings. The place didn't speak of wealth, it positively shouted out loud. There were more bathrooms than any family would ever need. Downstairs, he led them past an elegant library, billiards room, and glistening kitchen where several servants were working.

Williams took them down to the basement of his mansion. "What do you think of my wine cellar?"

Charles looked around. He was no connoisseur, but it seemed Williams clearly was.

"Now you'll see my favorite room of all." Williams opened another door with pride. "It's all state of the art in here. What do you think?"

The gleam of steel hurt his eyes and he blinked. Charles felt as if he were back in a gym, a sinister one, what with the black painted walls and bright overhead lights.

"What fabulous exercise equipment!" Barbara enthused.

Charles shuddered.

"It's the best money can buy. I work out here everyday."

"I don't blame you," Barbara said.

Charles saw nothing but evil devices of torture. It was cold in the room, very cold.

"Thanks for the tour and the dinner," Charles said. "We'll arrange to set up some meetings."

"We'll come separately," Barbara quickly interjected, "since we're dealing with separate legal matters."

"That'll be fine," Williams said, looking pleased, "and you feel free to use my private gym any time you like."

Charles quickly interjected, "Do you think you could come to our office? It would be a much more professional atmosphere."

"It's been getting harder for me to leave this place."

"That's no problem," Barbara responded with the compassion of Mother Teresa.

For a time, Charles didn't hear from Williams. He knew Barbara was going to the estate on a fairly regular basis, but he didn't bother asking her about it, and she didn't volunteer any information. Then one day, Barbara stopped by his office in the middle of the morning.

"Can you visit Vance Williams today?"

"Awfully short notice."

"He needs you. The police are harassing him."

"Why's that?"

Barbara gave him a tight smile. "His wife's car turned up in Florida with no sign of her. Pretty strange, huh?"

"What does Williams have to say?"

"Nothing at all. The police are kind of suspicious because of that incident when he lived down in Texas."

Charles fixed his gaze on Barbara. "What kind of incident?"

"Oh, just that he accidentally ran over and killed this friend of his."

For the next few weeks, Charles heard nothing more from Williams. His communication with Barbara was limited as well. They lived as strangers, rarely speaking. But Charles knew that Barbara was spending a good deal of time out at Williams's estate. There was more than one night when she didn't come home at all. Charles was fairly certain the relationship had gone way beyond the bounds of what could be considered professional.

"We're going to have to have a serious talk," he told her one evening when he found her in their condo. It was time to discuss a divorce. Charles wished now he'd insisted on a pre-nup. Then again, it hardly mattered, because he'd gladly give up half of everything he owned just to get out of a marriage that had become a living hell.

"Yes, I agree. We'll talk soon." Her voice was so sweet it could have given him diabetes. He was immediately on his guard.

He had the distinct impression that Barbara was making plans, plans he wouldn't particularly like.

A few days later, Guzman called him into the office. "How's it going with Williams?"

Charles shrugged. "I haven't heard from him lately. You should ask Barbara that question."

"She phoned a little while ago. She's out at his place now. Says Williams wants to see you again. They're going to send a car for you."

He groaned. "This is insulting and unprofessional, and it wastes a lot of my time."

"I have two words for you: billable hours. We're billing up the kazoo for your time and Barbara's. So take a nap in the car and relax. You're being well paid to do so."

The entire drive, all Charles could think about was how much he wanted to end his marriage. Barbara would be there. He would talk to her privately.

The door was answered by the same unsavory character. He gave Charles a hard look.

"I'm here to see Mr. Williams."

"This way," came the gruff reply.

Charles followed him downstairs to the basement level. The cold entered his bones almost immediately. Charles found himself back in the exercise room. And there was Barbara, waiting for him.

"Thank you, Monroe." The large man who reminded him of a Kodiak bear nodded and left.

"Where's Williams?"

"Busy."

"I don't understand. I came all this distance for what purpose?"

"Well, you did say you wanted to talk. I think now is the perfect time."

"I couldn't agree more. I think we should talk about a divorce."

She gave him a tight little smile. "Divorce isn't the answer I've come up with." Suddenly, without any warning, Barbara was holding up a gun. Light glistened off the steel barrel.

Charles gaped at her in shock. "What the hell do you think you're doing?"

"I'm going to kill you." She said the words without any display of emotion whatever.

"I'm willing to give you half of everything I own in a divorce settlement. Put the weapon away. Don't be insane."

"The thing is, I've decided I want everything you have. Vance thinks it's a good idea. I might marry him. I might not."

"What has Williams got to do with this?"

"He shot his wife with this very gun. Then he had Monroe cut up her body into small pieces and ground it into the concrete mixer. She made a contribution to his new swimming pool."

Charles felt as if he were going to throw up. "You have any idea how sick that is?"

"I thought it was pretty clever. Monroe drove her car down to Florida and abandoned it in a shopping mall. No one's ever going to know what happened to her."

"He told you that?"

"Client-attorney privilege. So Charles, before I kill you, I have one request. I want to watch you use the exercise equipment down here."

This was getting weirder by the second. "You get some perverse pleasure from that?"

She pointed to one of the shiny machines located on a mat. "That one's called an all-around trainer. Strap yourself in and get it started."

He studied the contraption. No way was he going to use it. She probably wanted to move up the control switch to the point where he'd suffer a major heart attack. Then she wouldn't have to shoot him at all. It would just appear as if he died of natural causes.

"I'm not helping you kill me."

"Then I will just have to shoot you." She raised the weapon, and there was no question in his mind that she was about to use it on him.

All of a sudden, he heard a noise, loud, thunderous. It sounded as if an earthquake had hit. The cellar certainly shook as though one had. Barbara was startled, losing her composure. Charles realized this was the only chance he would ever have to save himself. He rushed her, grabbing for the weapon.

They struggled; she was strong, no doubt about it. But as she fought with him, Barbara moved backwards for leverage and ended up tripping on the very device of torture she'd wanted to put him into. Charles tried again to snatch the gun from her hands while she was off-balance, but it went off.

The gunshot caught Barbara in the side. For just a moment, Charles thought of leaving her there to bleed to death, but it was just a momentary lapse. He was far from perfect, but he considered himself a civilized human being.

"I'll get some help for you," he said.

He took the weapon with him as a precaution, went upstairs, flipping open his cell phone and called 911, requesting an ambulance.

Monroe came toward him.

"I'm leaving," Charles said.

But Monroe wasn't listening. He had a dazed expression on his face. "Mr. Williams was sitting by the pool when it burst like a dam without any warning. It just cracked apart. The pool split open and the water gushed out. He's dead. The pool, it drowned Mr. Williams. It was a freak thing. Happened so fast, I couldn't save him."

Charles thought of Williams's wife, the woman killed and buried in the concrete. She had, in an ironic way, contributed to the creation of that pool. If there was any justice, her spirit finally got revenge and maybe a modicum of peace.

Could she have somehow haunted the pool? He didn't normally think that way. He was a man of logic and reason, not given to fanciful thoughts. Yet it did seem like a strange coincidence, the pool bursting just as Barbara was about to murder him in the same way that Williams had killed his wife.

Did that really matter? He was still alive. That was the important thing. He knew of only one way to honor the memory of the dead woman. Charles flipped his cell phone open again. Time he had a serious talk with those detectives. He could and would share what Barbara had told him. He'd be leaving this place with a police escort.

THE SHOCKING AFFAIR OF THE STEAMSHIP FRIESLAND

by Jack Grochot

My friend Sherlock Holmes was, in a word, irregular in his habits of late, so it was a cause of a little concern when, at our usual lunch-time together, for three days in a row, he excused himself and went up to his bedroom. On each occasion, he returned to our sitting room about two o'clock with nothing to say and with a dour look on his lanky face.

As in most instances, Holmes revealed the reason for his odd behaviour at a time of his own choosing. It was during lunch on the fourth day. We both were seated at the table, to which Mrs Hudson, our landlady, had brought a crock of piping-hot beef barley soup and a loaf of fresh-baked whole wheat bread. "Our neighbor, the smithy, whose activities I have been observing through my bedroom window," said Holmes, "is apparently dissatisfied with his earnings at the forge. He has taken up a sideline, odds-making, and collects wagers from his clients every day between noon and two o'clock at the blacksmith shop."

Ordinarily, this would have been a matter that fell under the exclusive jurisdiction of a fire-and-brimstone preacher, lecturing about the dangers of the vices. Holmes, however, had made it his business because of a request from an elderly lady, a friend of Mrs Hudson. The old woman had asked Holmes to determine why her husband owed a substantial sum of money to the blacksmith when, in fact, her spouse did not own a horse. She believed the blacksmith was taking the money for some sinful purpose, and she wanted her husband to stay out of it.

"Watson, this frisky lady is my rival," said Holmes. "She followed her husband to the blacksmith's without either of them knowing she was onto their scent. She witnessed a transaction between the two, and she has deduced correctly that there is some devilish conduct involved. Why did she need me at all? To tell her,

I suppose, that her husband is an addicted gambler and to confirm her suspicions about the blacksmith. I think that for my fee I shall demand one of her renowned blueberry cakes. It's an appropriate payment in light of the delicious meals I have missed on her behalf."

"Hold that thought," said I, looking out the window, "because we are about to have a visitor. A matronly woman has just stepped down from a four-wheeler and is approaching our door."

Mrs Hudson, after answering the bell, ascended the stairs to announce that Miss Mufalda Maker was down in the hall asking for Mr Sherlock Holmes.

"Send her up in three minutes, Mrs Hudson," instructed Holmes, still wearing his purple dressing gown. He went to his bedroom and changed into his brown gabardine trousers, white cotton shirt, and green wool jacket.

"Please come in and make yourself comfortable," said Holmes when Miss Maker appeared in the doorway.

"I am bashful about this, Mr Holmes," she answered, seating herself on the settee.

"Now, now, Miss Maker," Holmes said to reassure her, "there is no need to feel awkward. Whatever story you have to tell cannot be any more self deprecating than other stories that have been told within these walls."

Miss Maker was attired for business. She wore a charcoal grey, broad-brimmed felt hat with a black feather. Her jacket was checkered black and white with a fuzzy black fringe, and her dress was light grey with lace trim at the neck. The clothing and her bearing complemented the rest of her appearance. She had short-cropped straight brown hair that protruded slightly from beneath the hat, high cheek bones, full lips, and sullen brown eyes that darted between the two of us.

Holmes introduced me as a friend who assisted him in some of his investigations, and then his attention was drawn to her hands and her clothes.

"You are a seamstress, I see, one who designs what she makes."

"Why, yes, but how on earth did you know?"

"It is a peculiarity of mine, Miss Maker. I have made a study of how the hands can give away a person's occupation. Your right forefinger, for instance, shows the mark of a needle prick, which you must have inflicted accidentally upon yourself today. But I confess that I have seen the sign above your shop in the Strand. 'Mafalda Maker, Seamstress and Designer,' it reads, if my memory serves me correctly."

"It sounds simple now that you have explained it."

"I have vowed in the past to stop explaining myself, and this is the last time I shall do it," said Holmes with a wry smile, charming her in his special way with women. "Our digression has made your visit a deeper mystery."

"Then I shall tell my story, although it does embarrass me to do so," said she, glancing at the floor. "I received a parcel by messenger yesterday. I had been expecting one because I had ordered four dozen tulip bulbs from Holland to plant in my garden this fall. Imagine my surprise when I opened the box and found not tulip bulbs but money—ten bundles of American one hundred dollar bills, a hundred bills to a bundle. It was more money than I had ever seen at any one time."

"Your situation," Holmes interjected, "reminds me of a case Dr Watson and I successfully resolved last year, one in which the postman delivered to a lady, single like yourself, a cardboard box containing two freshly-severed human ears. Let us hope the conclusion of your puzzle is far less grisly than that of Miss Cushing, of Cross Street, Croydon."

"I recall reading about that episode in the newspaper, Mr Holmes," continued Miss Maker, "but I do not remember the mention of your name in connection with it. I believe it was an inspector from Scotland Yard who solved the crime, a murder by a jealous lover, I think."

Sherlock Holmes looked disappointed. "If pressed, Inspector Lestrade would concede that I made a noteworthy contribution to the Yard in the Croydon affair. He has a penchant for attracting all the attention in the dailies," Holmes said after some hesitation. "Yet again we digress. Please go on with your narrative."

"Of course. When I saw what was in the package, I had no idea what to do, Mr Holmes. I had no one to ask for advice. I thought about notifying the police, but decided to wait until after I had spoken with one of the solicitors on Bond Street whose wife I sew for.

"Later in the evening, my plans were changed by a man who came to my door. He was polite and professional in his manner after he identified himself as Inspector Athelney Jones of Scotland Yard. He was also quite emphatic. He wanted to take custody of the money, for the bills were counterfeit and he needed them for his inquiry. Naturally, I complied and handed over the hundred thousand dollars, believing it was worthless. He placed the bundles inside a canvas bag he had brought with him.

"I thought it queer that he didn't require me to hand over the box and wrapper, but I said nothing about them and he left. I asked him first how he knew I had received the package. That was classified information, he said, and it would come out in court.

"The longer I thought about it, Mr Holmes, the more strange the circumstances seemed, and it became even more so today. After conferring with the solicitor, a Mr Henry Daubner, I called upon Inspector Jones so I could ask him the questions that have occurred to me since his abrupt visit. You can probably picture the alarm on my face when I was shown to the desk of Inspector Jones and saw an altogether different person than the one who knocked at my apartment door. Insisting that there must be some mistake, I was assured there was no other Athelney Jones at Scotland Yard and that the man who took the money must have been an imposter."

Holmes realized that she had finished and so he guided the conversation with a question. "Would you kindly describe the man who came to your door?"

"He was tall and thin, like yourself, Mr Holmes. He was balding with salt and pepper hair on the sides of his head. I would estimate that he was fifty years old. He had a Vandyke beard, rounded shoulders, sallow skin and penetrating, icy-blue eyes that were close together against a long, beak-like nose. I gave this description to the real Inspector Jones, who promised to look into the matter. He was very interested in the box and the wrapper, I might add, but they were thrown out with the trash."

"And what is it that you would have me do, Miss Maker?" asked Holmes.

Miss Maker said Jones had recommended that she engage Holmes's services to recover any reward that might be offered for the return of the money to its rightful owner. "Inspector Jones doubted my caller had a lawful claim to the sum," said Miss Maker.

Miss Maker, in response to another question, recalled that the parcel came from Johanssen Flowers of 1425 Etna Avenue, Strotherdam, South Holland, the Netherlands.

"Were there no tulip bulbs at all in the package?" asked Holmes.

"No, none, just a few dried skins of tulip bulbs."

"And the flaps on the top of the box, were they loose or glued shut when you received it?"

"They were loose, I am sure."

"Those two facts tell us a great deal," declared Holmes. "They tell us that the box was unwrapped and opened in transit and that the money was not placed there by the sender. Someone between the sender and yourself, Miss Maker, broke the seal, removed the contents, replaced them with the money, and re-wrapped the parcel. Did you save the string by any chance?"

"No, I tossed it out with the trash also."

"Pity, for I might have been able to learn some things from the knots, as I did in the case of the severed ears," said Holmes. "Perhaps you can retrieve the box, the wrapper, and the string from the trash bin," he added hopefully.

"No, the trash was collected this morning, Mr Holmes," said Miss Maker.

"Well, Miss Maker, this case is of interest to me because it has some uncommon aspects that could be instructive," said Holmes. "In addition, there is the obvious possibility that you have been drawn into some criminal affair. Otherwise, why the substitution of the money for the tulip bulbs and why the charade by the bogus Inspector Jones? Unfortunately, we have less to go on than in the Croydon matter. Nonetheless, I shall do what I am able to keep you clear of scandal. I shall be in touch."

The gaslights were being lit outside, so Holmes asked me to escort Miss Maker to the street, where I hailed a cab for her. Once she was on her way home, he and I walked to Cavendish Square for a nice meal at a new Greek restaurant we both had wanted to try. Over a dish of hummus and unleavened bread for an appetizer, we discussed Miss Maker's experience and came to the conclusion that if she had not given up the money, the man probably was prepared to do her harm. For the rest of the meal, Holmes talked of concerts, performers, boxing matches, the microscopic differences in animal blood compared to human blood, and the gauge of the wheels on the new Victoria carriage, which leaves a print in the dirt more narrow than the brougham or the hansom.

The fall air was distinctly cooler on the walk back to Baker Street, so we decided to have a fire when once we were inside. We finished our cigars at the same time that we got to our lodgings, and we spent a pleasant night at home. Little did we know that the events Holmes had undertaken to investigate would nearly cost us both our lives.

The next morning Holmes had gone off on a line of inquiry before I came down to breakfast. I had plenty of time to complete several pages of a manuscript before he came through the door. "I have wasted most of the day trying to single out the messenger service that delivered the parcel to Miss Maker," Holmes complained. "But I was successful at last when I inquired at McPherson and Son, Limited, in Barclay Square. Their records for the day before yesterday showed a delivery to 122a Church Street, and Miss Maker's signature was on the slip. The origin of the package was shown to be the Dutch steamship *Friesland*, which is docked at Southampton. Persistence, my dear Watson, is a virtue that at times out-does ingenuity in the art of detection. Now, I would be obliged if my chronicler accompanied me to Southampton, both to relieve the boredom of traveling alone and to take note of the twists and turns of an investigation when it seems to have come to a dead end."

We took a cab to the train station at Charing Cross and arrived in the port city about an hour later. We located the *Friesland* easily and went up the gangway to the main deck, where stevedores were loading cargo in preparation for the ship's departure. The *Friesland* was both a cargo and a passenger vessel. Holmes sought out the first mate, James Woodson, who spoke English, and furnished him with a card. Woodson was leery initially, but he warmed to Holmes's friendly approach. Even so, he answered questions cautiously. Holmes explained that he was trying to find the rightful owner of a large amount of money that had been transported aboard the ship. This seemed to put the seaman at ease completely. In response to a question, he told Holmes that the ship had made a voyage from New York City to Rotterdam, its home port, and then on to Southampton. It next was sailing back to New York.

"There is a man who might be of assistance but whose name I do not know," said Holmes, and he described the caller who impersonated Athelney Jones.

"Ah, the nose and those eyes," replied the first mate. "That could be no one other than Mr. Bracken, who boarded the *Friesland* in New York. I remember him because he had some valuables that he wanted to store in the ship's safe. What they were he did not specify, but I informed him we had no safe large enough to accommodate the belongings of our passengers. He became annoyed and threatened to file an action against the owners of the ship if he were robbed."

Holmes requested to see the passenger manifest to determine Bracken's first name. It was shown to be William and it further revealed that he had booked passage to Southampton.

"Would it be possible, Mr Woodson," Holmes wanted to know, "for any person aboard this ship to gain access to the cargo hold?"

"It would be possible, for the area is not locked, but I can't imagine why anyone would want to do that," the first mate answered.

"Certain people have motives that are sometimes beyond the imagination," Holmes observed. "Was Mr Bracken traveling alone?"

"As far as I know he was alone. I saw him associate with no other passenger, and he occupied a compartment with a single bed."

Finished with the interview, Holmes left the ship and found a telegraph office to send a wire to a private detective in New York, John Joyce, for whom Holmes once had done a favour. The wire asked Joyce to make inquiries of the authorities to ascertain whether William Bracken was wanted for a crime and whether any criminal act had been committed recently involving a hundred thousand dollars in hundred dollar bills. The wire contained a description of the man believed to be Bracken.

On the train back to Charing Cross, Holmes speculated as to why Bracken would have deposited the money into the parcel. "Obviously, he was aware of an enemy watching him. Perhaps because he had been careless and allowed himself to be seen with the cash. Whatever the reason, Watson, he was fearful enough to separate himself from the money, clever enough to conceal it from his adversary, and bold enough to deceive Miss Maker so he could make off with a fortune into the recesses of Greater London. We are dealing here with a seasoned manipulator."

"And finding him now," said I, "will be more difficult than locating the proverbial needle in the haystack."

"All is not so hopeless," remarked Holmes. "No investigation ever comes to a standstill unless one's determination is lacking. Tomorrow I shall call upon the currency exchange counters at the major banks and see if anyone matching his description has tendered large denominations of American money. Perhaps the merchants of Fleet Street can point us in the direction of Mr William Bracken."

To our amazement, when we returned to our apartment, Miss Maker was there waiting for us. She was horribly disfigured. Her right eye was swollen shut and there was a bruise on her left cheek. Her lower lip was cut and turgid.

"Oh, Mr Holmes," she moaned, relieved to see him. "They thought I was his confederate and beat me so I would tell them where I had hidden the money."

"Come, come now, Miss Maker, start at the beginning, please," Holmes encouraged, and patted her on the back. Meanwhile, I fetched a basin and poured out some dark vinegar to treat her wounds.

"I was on my way to my shop this morning," she related, "and when I shut my door and was about to lock it, two men, ruffians they were, came out of nowhere in the hallway and forced me back inside. They said they had been watching me ever since Mr Bracken—that's what they called him—had come to see me. They had followed him to my flat and they said they knew he gave the money to me to hide. They wanted me to tell them where it was. When I told them I had given the money to the man who called at my door, they began to strike me. One of them held me while the other with the tattoo on his forearm struck me in the face, again and again. They then ransacked my quarters after warning me not to make a sound. A lot of good that would have done anyway, because my landlord, who lives upstairs, is practically deaf. When they were satisfied that the money wasn't anywhere to be found, they departed, cautioning me against calling the police. I disregarded them and notified a constable, who contacted Inspector Jones. He took down their descriptions and said he would investigate immediately. After I straightened up my apartment, I came here. I'm afraid to go back there, Mr Holmes, in the event they're waiting for me."

"Don't worry about that," Holmes instructed her. "Dr Watson and I will go back with you, but not before Dr Watson tends to your injuries. Once you are back inside your apartment, lock the door and don't open it for anyone. You'll be quite safe. Now, if you don't mind repeating, would you describe these thugs for me?"

"The one who beat me about the face was stout with a big belly. He was about forty years old.

"He had a broad nose, bulbous eyes, a knit cap, and rotten front teeth. He was not very tall, a little taller than I. The other, who held me, was bigger and did most of the talking. He wore a pea jacket and a knit cap as well. His eyes were sunken and his mouth was wide. He was about forty also."

"What was the tattoo on the forearm of the one who struck you?"

"It was a mermaid holding an anchor."

We accompanied Miss Maker home and made sure she was safely inside before leaving. On the way back to Baker Street, Holmes suggested that the attackers came from the *Friesland* because they apparently had followed Bracken from the time he left the ship. Holmes guessed they were crewmen, based on the particulars supplied by Miss Maker.

"I doubt, Watson," said he, "that Inspector Jones has made any connections between the parcel and the *Friesland*, or between Bracken and the men who attacked Miss Maker. So, first thing tomorrow, we shall make a trip to Scotland Yard to share the information. I prefer to work independently, but in this instance only the official detective police force can bring to justice the miscreants who assaulted Miss Maker."

The next morning, after hearing the results of Holmes's investigation, Inspector Jones, his eyes twinkling, expressed appreciation for the evidence but he questioned Holmes's intent. "Do you want the credit for solving the assault upon Miss Maker or do you have designs on the money, or is it both?" Jones pried.

"The credit belongs to you entirely, for it is you who would benefit most from the favourable publicity," Holmes answered with some indignation. "As for the money, we have no clue yet as to the rightful owner, so the question of a reward is still an open one."

The solution to the mystery of the money, however, awaited Holmes upon our return to Baker Street. Mrs Hudson had accepted delivery of a telegram from John Joyce, the private detective in New York City. He reported startling news about Bracken and the money. Bracken, said Joyce, was an alias for an international malefactor from London, one Daniel Garber, who had formed a gang in New York City to kidnap a wealthy businessman. The gang had demanded one hundred thousand dollars ransom. Once it was paid, Garber gave the slip to the authorities, double-crossed his recruits, and made off with the loot, leaving them for the police to capture. All but one of them was caught. Once in custody, the others named Garber as their leader. There was no more evidence against him, though, so the police would be gratified, according to the telegram, to have Garber found in possession of the ransom money. The bills were marked, the telegram said.

Holmes and I took a cab back to Scotland Yard, only to learn that Jones already had gone with some constables to the *Friesland* to arrest the men responsible for the attack on Miss Maker. Holmes put a sheet of foolscap into Jones's typewriter and left him a detailed note about the villain we knew as Bracken. Holmes and I spent the remainder of the morning and part of the afternoon alerting the clerks at currency exchange counters about the marked hundred dollar bills. None had been negotiated so far. The clerks were given a description of Bracken, or Garber, and told to notify Holmes or Inspector Jones if an attempt was made to exchange the money.

After we had finished at the last of the banks, we returned to Scotland Yard, where we found Miss Maker seated next to Jones's desk. She was looking refreshed and was excited to have identified the men who had beaten her. Jones was working on a report.

"They do not deny what they did, Mr Holmes, but they say they know nothing of the whereabouts of Garber," said Jones. "It is their contention that they stopped following him after he entered Miss Maker's apartment. They say they are sure he left the money with her. Maybe a few days in the dock will make them want to change their tune."

The day was a satisfying one, despite the lack of progress on locating the ransom money. Holmes and I escorted Miss Maker home once again and went back to our own apartment afterward. Mrs Hudson had prepared a pot roast with fresh vegetables for supper, and we enjoyed that with a glass of port. Later, Holmes, still seated at the table, took a long drag on his cigarette and marveled at the restraint shown by Garber in not cashing in at least some of the booty.

"There is a reason for him to act contrary to what would be normal," said Holmes. "It is the absence of normal behaviour that is the key to this mystery."

There was soon more to add to this conundrum.

We were disturbed in our reading of the evening papers by a strong ring of the bell and a clamour of footsteps on the stairs. "It is someone desperate for help, if I am not much mistaken," said Holmes as he opened the door to greet a breathless Athelney Jones.

"Mr Holmes, can you and Dr Watson come with me to the Carlton Private Hotel on Harley Street?"

"What is it, Jones?"

"It seems that the two birds who manhandled Miss Maker have no end to their violent ways. Your Mr Bracken, Garber, has been found dead, murdered. We're sure it is he because of the description, plus he registered at the establishment using his given name. His skull has been bashed in, and the canvas bag he carried to Miss Maker's is on the bed, empty. There was a terrible struggle in the room and it would be helpful if you used your keen eyes to make a sweep of the place and give us the benefit of your advice."

I was on my feet in an instant, not even taking time to fold the newspaper. Holmes and I grabbed our jackets off the rack and were out on the street with Jones before he could say another word. The cab he had waiting took us to the hotel in less than a half hour, but by this time there was a crowd of curiosity seekers milling about the entrance. The manager was standing in the hallway talking to two constables. He stopped in mid-sentence and climbed the stairs to the second floor beside the inspector, saying how the expected publicity would be bad for business. "There's nothing I can do to discourage the press from writing about it," Jones told him.

Room 211 looked as if a locomotive had passed through it. Every stick of furniture was upset except the bed, but the mattress and box springs were partially on the floor because the slats had been knocked off the frame. Curled in a corner near an upturned writing table was the man with the beak-like nose, a grotesque expression on his face. The side of his head was blood-soaked from a wicked blow by a blunt object. He was wearing a lightweight frock coat, indicating that he had just come in from outside when the ruckus occurred.

Holmes began at once to examine the body, taking his usual methodical approach. Then he started in the corner where the victim lay and worked his way clockwise around the room close to the walls. "Halloa! A button from a waistcoat, and not Garber's," said he, picking up the object from under an overturned armchair. At the center of the room he came across a glass paperweight and announced that he had discovered the murder weapon, noting a perfect palm print in the dried blood covering most of the surface.

"It matters not which of our two sailors dealt the blow, they are both equally culpable in this crime," said Jones. "Garber was a ne'er-do-well, but I shall see them swing for this just the same."

"Don't be too sure of your case against them," Holmes warned, but he declined to explain. He continued his slow exploration of the room, which involved setting the furniture upright, one piece at a time. "The absence of any footprints, due to the dry weather, is a distinct disadvantage," said he as he stood a bench on its legs again. It was the last piece of furniture needing to be turned upright. "There is nothing more to learn here," said he, finally.

The constables on the scene had gone up and down the hall on all three floors to locate anyone who heard or saw anything. The chambermaid who found the body in the evening said she had been in the room about the same time the previous day and nothing was awry then. One tenant in the adjoining room said he thought he heard thumping noises coming from the direction of Room 211 in the late afternoon. He said he looked out to see a man leaving. The tenant said he only saw the back of the man in the hallway and remembered he carried a satchel. The man was wearing plaid trousers, a blue waistcoat and tan gaiters. Jones pressed the witness to be sure there was only the one man walking in the hallway and not two. "There was only the one," the tenant said, recalling that the man had flaxen hair plastered down, bushy side-whiskers, was about six feet tall and weighed about two hundred pounds.

We accompanied Jones back to headquarters, where Holmes asked to speak with the two culprits in the beating of Miss Maker. Jones took Holmes down to the lockup and opened the outer door after explaining to the guard that Holmes was assisting Scotland Yard in an investigation. The pair had just finished eating supper, a bowl of fish chowder with bread, when Holmes approached their cell.

After he introduced himself, Holmes apprised them that Inspector Jones was prepared to charge them with the murder of the man they knew as Bracken.

"Please, please, Mr Holmes, help us," said the one with the big belly and decayed teeth. "We'll take our medicine for what we did to the woman, but please don't let him pin a killing on us, too."

"I shall do what I am able," said Holmes. "You can help yourselves by telling me if Bracken associated with anyone aboard the *Friesland.*"

"He had no friends that I am aware of," said the other assailant. "He kept to himself."

"I saw him talking to another passenger once," said the fat sailor. "He was a man who also came aboard in New York. His name I never heard, but it was a lively discussion, for the other man was waving his arms and shaking his head no."

"Describe him."

"He was about twenty-five years old, flaxen hair plastered down, bushy side-whiskers, big round eyes, maybe six feet tall and two hundred pounds or so."

Holmes got all he could from the pair, then went back up to Jones's desk.

"I doubt these boys know anything about what went on in Room 211," said Holmes to the tired inspector. "I hope you consider the probability of another killer."

"I am considering it enough that I will not charge them with the murder tonight," responded Jones. "A good night's sleep will give me fresh perspective tomorrow."

"Then I bid you a good night," said Holmes.

"It has been a long day, and I am wishing for a good night," said Jones as we parted company.

Once again back in our rooms, Holmes was contemplative and seemed to gain buoyancy by using me as a sounding board for his train of thought, a purpose that I served on many occasions and one for which he had complimented me several times. He had changed into his mouse-coloured dressing gown and was perched in an armchair with his knees drawn up to his chin, smoking a cherry-wood pipe, a comical sight that reminded me of a giant owl perched in the crook of a tree branch. I joined him with a pipe full of my favourite Arcadia mixture.

"Our deceased gang leader, Watson, feared more than the two seamen in Jones's lockup," said Holmes. "He might not even have known of their interest in him. It was his accomplice in the kidnapping, the man he betrayed and who eluded the police—that was who troubled him."

"But surely he worried about the authorities, too," I interjected.

"Yes, but he knew if they were an imminent threat they would have put him in irons before the ship left New York Harbour. Is it not more plausible that the one gang member boarded the ship and was waiting for the opportunity to overtake him? An attack aboard ship would have been unpropitious because the list of suspects would be short. He waited until the ship docked and the two of them were far from it."

"If the killer followed Garber to the hotel, he must have seen him stop at Miss Maker's."

"Yes, but he was not so easily fooled into believing, like our sailor friends, that she had been entrusted to hide the money."

The hour was late, so I knocked out my pipe and retired, leaving Holmes in the armchair, deep in thought.

When I finished with my toilet in the morning and had gone down to breakfast, Holmes was pacing in front of the sofa, still clad in his dressing gown from the night before. "How could I have been such an idiot, Watson?" he pleaded, with self-loathing. "The fact that no one has attempted to exchange the dollars for pounds tells us something of great significance. Why could I not have seen it before this? I hope we are not too late." He implored me to go with him to Southampton and to hope we arrived there before the *Friesland* set sail for America.

"Consider me in on your plans," I told him, oblivious to what lay ahead.

"Put your service revolver in your pocket—we might need your sure aim," he cautioned, reaching into a drawer of the sideboard for his own weapon, a five-shot Walther.

On the way to Charing Cross, we stopped to take Jones along. Holmes spent an interminable amount of time persuading him to accompany us to the ship. Jones was reluctant because he said there was insufficient evidence to arrest anyone, particularly someone whose name was unknown and whose connection to the crime was tenuous at best. Nonetheless, he came along, with the understanding that there would be no official action unless the man Holmes confronted confessed to the murder.

"I fully expect to know his name before I confront him, and I am confident he will be in possession of the ransom money," Holmes predicted.

"Now that certainly will go a long way in changing my attitude," said Jones. "But be forewarned, Mr Holmes, I'm only going because in the past, once or twice, your hunches have produced the desired results."

The *Friesland* was still docked when we arrived in Southampton and it was not scheduled to leave port until four o'clock in the afternoon.

Holmes, Jones, and I waited at the top of the gangway while a deckhand went off to find Mr Woodson, the first mate, after Holmes requested to speak with him. The main deck had been cleared of cargo, and seamen were busy making preparations to set sail. Occasionally, passengers came aboard bearing luggage, checking in with a sailor holding a clipboard at the end of the gangway. He would match them to the names on his list and tell them the numbers of their cabins.

Woodson's demeanour had changed radically since Holmes spoke with him last. He was curt and uncooperative.

"What is it this time?" said he when he approached us.

"I presume you know Inspector Jones of Scotland Yard," said Sherlock Holmes.

"Of course I do," said Woodson. "He took two of my men and left me shorthanded with the cargo."

"And he is about to take one of your passengers," said Holmes, confidently.

"Which one?" Woodson asked.

"I can't tell you that until after you have shown me the old passenger manifest again and let me compare it to the new one on that clipboard," said Holmes, pointing to the sailor.

"I shall do nothing of the sort," Woodson bristled.

"Then I shall be back in two hours," said Jones, "with a writ and you will accompany me to headquarters in London with the manifest. If the ship sails without you, so be it."

"Wait here," said Woodson, reconsidering his position, and he turned to climb the steps toward the bridge.

To avoid looking conspicuous, the three of us engaged in idle conversation until Woodson returned. He handed the manifest to Holmes and called to the seaman with the clipboard to come to where we were gathered. Woodson took the clipboard and handed it to Holmes, too. Holmes examined it for some time, leafing through the pages with determination on his face. He appeared frustrated at one point and asked me to help him cross-reference the names by calling out those that were printed on the old manifest. When I came to the name Charles Wolker, he stopped me and announced: "That is it! He is on both manifests. This must be our man, the missing member of Garber's gang. He is not yet marked as being aboard." Jones suggested we go through the remaining names to make certain no others were duplicated. We found a married couple returning to New York, but that was all.

Holmes gave back the clipboard to the seaman checking in the passengers, with instructions that when Charles Wolker boarded, the seaman was to take off his hat. That would serve as a signal to us. So as not to attract attention to ourselves, we separated, taking up positions at different places on the main deck, all within sight of the sailor with the clipboard.

The wait seemed like an eternity. At irregular intervals, passengers would board the ship but the sailor kept his hat on his head. Every male passenger was scrutinized to see if he matched the description of Garber's killer, but each one passed us unchallenged. Holmes, Jones, and I would glance in one another's direction after the passengers came aboard just to make sure the description was off the mark, in case the sailor had forgotten his cue.

My pocket watch said twenty minutes to three when, at long last, a tall, muscular man with flaxen hair plastered down, carrying a satchel and one suitcase, hurried up the gangway.

He stopped to check in and I saw the sailor's right hand reach for his hat. I sprang forward, while Holmes and Jones went toward the man at the same time.

"Good afternoon, Mr Wolker," said Holmes as he introduced himself. "And this is Inspector Jones of Scotland—"

With one motion, Wolker dropped the suitcase, reached inside his coat, and produced a pistol. He did not hesitate before he pulled the trigger. I saw Jones fall to the deck as if his legs had turned to rubber. Holmes took several steps backward and I found cover behind a wooden railing. I had withdrawn my revolver from my coat pocket but could not return fire because there were people standing behind Wolker, stunned and unable to move. Holmes, from his angle, had a clear shot and took it, but not before Wolker squeezed off two more shots in Holmes's direction. He missed, but Holmes scored with a bullet in Wolker's chest.

Wolker did not fall, but retreated against the wall beneath the bridge. With no one in the background, I now had a clear shot and took it. Wolker went down onto the deck, face up. Holmes and I approached him with our revolvers pointed. Wolker tried to raise his pistol, but he fell back, dead. I checked for a pulse and could get none, so I left him and Holmes there and went to the aid of Jones. It was hopeless. The bullet had struck him square in the forehead, killing him instantly.

A crowd began to gather, and Woodson came down from the bridge with the captain to see what they could do to calm the passengers. I went back over to where Holmes was kneeling over Wolker's body counting the bundles of hundred dollar bills in the satchel. I told Holmes about Jones, and he said he had expected the worst because he had seen the wound.

"There was no attempt to exchange the bills for pounds, Watson," said Holmes, "because Garber, and later Wolker, intended to take the money back to America. My guess is either of them likely would have boarded a train in New York and gone to some other city where the police would have no suspicions."

The next day's newspapers were filled with praises for Jones, who was both mourned and credited with solving the murder of Garber and recovering the ransom money by downing the criminal who tried to escape with it. There was a vague mention of Holmes assisting Jones.

Scotland Yard communicated the developments to the New York Police Department and in return there was word that the family of the kidnapped businessman had offered a thousand dollar reward for the return of the ransom money. Miss Maker was ecstatic and offered to share the reward with Holmes, but he politely accepted his normal fee instead.

"You realize, my dear Watson," said he one evening afterward by the fire, "the hangman could not have achieved better results in the case of Mr Garber and Mr Wolker. Naturally, I regret the loss of Jones in the process, but seldom has the criminal element reaped its just desserts as in this instance.

"If Wolker had not reacted as he did, Jones would be here to bask in the glory, and I would have had the opportunity to confront Wolker with this." He held up the button he had found on the floor of Room 211. "It would have fit perfectly into the space from which it was torn on his waistcoat."

KILLING SAM CLEMENS

by William Burton McCormick

August, 1867, Odessa

"My theory of fiction," said Sam, sitting at the café table across from me, "is that there are no new stories. The same tales repeat generation to generation, civilization to civilization. Only the details change." He paused to taste his whiskey. "The modern author earns his keep only in the manner of his telling, Joe."

I smiled, sipped my cognac as Sam drank his Scotch. My name wasn't "Joe," but I wished him to think it was. "And our personal stories, Sam? The true ones, I mean. Are they as repetitive as fiction?"

"I think so. But who knows the roles we're assigned? That's where Providence will have her say…A smoke?"

"No, I'm trying to quit."

"I imagine you'll succeed. I quit every week." Sam struck a match, concentrated on lighting his cigar. As he did, I sized up this stranger across my table. Sam looked about my age, early thirties, dressed tolerably enough, nothing distinctive in his appearance really except a briar of unruly red hair and a bushy moustache. He talked more like a literary theorist than a routine travel writer with a few fiction publications to his credit.

In fact, it was his talking—and his use of English, rare as it is in Odessa—which had caught my attention at the harbor. Two Americans so far from home, we'd naturally struck up a conversation, then spent the afternoon in the café talking over spirits. I sensed Sam was growing a bit tipsy.

It would make him easier to rob.

"So, this 'frog tale' was quite a success?" I asked.

Sam blew smoke rings into the humid air. "It was."

"Published in New York?"

"Nationally."

An exaggeration? That's the trouble with artists, you seldom know. My last two swindles weren't worth the effort, and I had no hankering to repeat my mistakes. An American abroad should carry silver dollars or at least rubles here in the Russian Empire, but as a writer he might be flat broke. I certainly had never heard of Samuel Clemens.

I rubbed my bad knee beneath the table. It'd been a month since the Spaniard's wallet brought any livable monies. And I had to kill him to get it.

Sam checked his pocket watch—silver plated, a good sign—then frowned. "I've two hours 'till my ship leaves. I'm sorry to say, we should adjourn this gathering, Joe."

Well, here's the moment then. The watch was proof enough, I guess.

A pity, Sam had wit.

"There's a church near here," I said as deftly as I could. "It might make an interesting account for your readers back in San Francisco."

"I've seen a half-dozen…"

"Yes, but this one has the most astonishing display of artifacts. The works are exquisite, beyond anything I've seen." I pushed my cognac away, it would be best to be sober. "They say these relics are from the days of Olga and Prince Vladimir themselves. It's your duty as a travel writer to relay such wonders to your readers, isn't it?"

He frowned. "If we hurry, the harbor's a ways off…"

"Twenty minutes, Sam. It's all the time we need."

We soon arrived at Pokrovskaya Cathedral, a square-ish white-marble structure dominating a small park off the city center. At the sight of the cathedral's golden dome, Sam shuffled through his shoulder bag, withdrawing a leather-bound notebook into which he scribbled:

Spire-topped roof resembles a great bronze turnip turned up-side down.

I felt my brow furl. "Do editors pay for such observations?" I asked.

"Six cents a page." He said smugly and shoved the notebook back into the bag.

Of course. *Six cents for nothing.*

I aptly praised Sam's hard-earned skills and harkened him through the opened door of the cathedral. The interior was even grander than the exterior, snow-white marble inlaid with gold and bronze, the icons of a dozen Orthodox saints peering down from above. A small crowd was gathered near the altar, several black-clad priests among them, but these holy men were not the center of attention. All eyes were upon a small choir just beginning their hymns.

Caps in hands, Sam and I stood there quietly as they sang. Their hymns began as a barely audible hum, expanding to an ethereal chant that rose over several minutes to superhuman strength. An army of invisible angels joined in, the chorus's power turning tenfold. It was a marvelous performance, perhaps the best I had known, marred only towards the end by an elderly man in the congregation, a decrepit and destitute-looking fellow whose fits of coughing nearly brought the piece to an early close.

Still Sam was moved. "I am not a great admirer of organized religions," said he. "But that was truly inspiring. As fine a choir as I've ever heard."

"They sing everyday at this hour. There will be an encore, several in fact." I lit two votive candles, handed one to Sam. "But your ship will not wait and there is much to see."

"Where are these artifacts?"

"In a vault below. Come."

We hurried out the rear of the cathedral to a shaded yard loosely separated from the surrounding park by a crumbling white-stone wall. There was an antiquity in this secluded garden, the shadows of the Ottomans hanging in the air. Among the scattered stones we found a series of weathered steps leading down into the earth, the opening of a tunnel just visible.

"There, Sam." I said. "Our passage to the vaults is within."

At this entrance, I slowed to a read a notice affixed to the keystone. Two children—a boy and a girl—had been lost in these tunnels weeks ago. By order of Odessa's governor, all known entrances to the catacombs were to be sealed in a month's time to prevent further tragedy.

I paused, trying to calculate the days since posting.

"It is out of date," said a priest who had trailed us into the yard. He reached up, tore the paper from the stone. "I should have done this much earlier."

"What do you mean, Father?"

"The children are safe. They found their way out a day after this sign was hung." He smiled. "To emerge unharmed, when the search parties had given up, a miracle."

"Yes, a miracle."

"What is happening?" asked Sam, rather flustered and reminding me he knew no Russian.

"Two children were lost briefly, but now are home. We can go."

The priest started to protest our path, but I turned away, ushered Sam down the steps. We felt the drop in temperature as we reached the bottom, the air so much cooler than the burning summer surface. As always, I regretted the absence of a coat.

I glanced at my companion. Sam stoically squinted behind that candle, the flame light sparkling in his narrowed eyes, his attention focused on the high-but-narrow white-stone corridor stretching ahead.

"This tunnel is just one of many, Sam. These are the largest catacombs in the world, greater than those of Paris and Rome combined. Men who journey inside are often lost forever. It's a wonder those children found their way out."

"Where is the vault?"

"A little ways on. Not far." I motioned ahead with my free hand. "The path is straight, we'll have no trouble."

Sam held his watch up to the candle flame. "My ship leaves in a little over an hour."

"We'll have you on the surface in ten minutes. You can get a carriage-for-hire. I know a driver who is usually at the corner this hour."

"You visit this cathedral often?"

"Four times before. You will be the fifth."

He grew quiet. We probed the darkness in silence. With every step our light forced back the gloom, the spectral-white tunnels extending forever, our two candles birthing four shadows to keep us company.

"These passages are surprisingly sterile." I said when we were some fifty yards inside. "I've never seen a rat, seldom glimpsed a bat. Even insects are rare. Lifeless, it's like tunnels inside the moon."

"And as cold."

"Well, this may warm your soul, Sam." I knocked on the dusty wall. "We are directly beneath the cathedral, and the choir above will sing momentarily. It is even more magnificent down here. I am no architect—I know nothing of acoustics—but their voices are magnified inside this tunnel. It is as if the hymns are piped from Heaven itself, Sam. Overpowering, amazing, awe-inspiring, I have seen stalwart atheists brought to tears."

"I would welcome such rapture, if it occurs."

"Worthy of your travel reports, yes? You will send me a clipping from your newspaper in San Francisco?"

"If it is as thrilling as you say."

"It will be."

I motioned ahead. In a matter of a few steps, we reached the spot where the Spaniard had died. "*No mas. No mas,*" he'd screamed, his cries drowned out by the chorus above. I had walked back innocently through the cathedral afterwards, no suspicious glances from priest or congregation, even pausing to put three useless Spanish half céntimos in the tithe box.

But only three. *No mas.*

I slowed my steps, let Sam grow closer. When the choir sings…

A strange notion entered my head then. Perhaps it was the familiarity of the scene, but I thought of Sam's theory that all stories repeat. How many murders—real or imagined—had occurred in the murk of dungeons such as this? I recalled a favorite.

"Have you read, 'The Cask of Amontillado,' Sam?"

"I'm no friend of the Dark Romantics."

"But have you read it?"

"Yes. And I can't abide the ending. The murderer gets off Scot free."

"Indeed. It is one of my pet tales. The two men winding through the gloom of the catacombs, much like us."

"The end of similarities, I'd hope."

"Yes."

We laughed, though I longer than him. We were as friends. I knew the roles now, no Providence needed. I was the trusted Montresor leading Sam's Fortunato down to his doom as in Poe's tale.

This cheered me greatly. It was all black theater, wasn't it? As he said, only the details change.

"Is this vault near?" he asked.

"It's just beyond the archway, Sam. Can you see it?"

"No."

"There." I pointed to a small opening at the end of the corridor. "It's the width of a man and half the height. We can just squeeze through."

He muttered something, gritting his teeth, a skeptic by nature. Beyond the archway, I would do it. Choir or not, we would be too far in, I hoped, to be heard.

"Here we are," I said as I ducked under the low arch. "You will marvel at the beauty on this side, Sam."

"I should hope it's worth the effort."

"My hope as well." I shoved my candle into a nearby crevice, blew it out. "Ah, I've lost the flame." I shouted from the other side. "Will you help me relight it?"

Crouching in the darkness, I pulled the knife from my pocket, and waited for Sam to emerge through the gap.

A backlit silhouette appeared in the opening—I stabbed—but struck only cloth, his bag pitched ahead of him as he tried to force his body under the archway. The power lost, the blade ripped up to Sam's shoulder, grazing him and severing his carrying strap. The bag fell between us. Sam shoved me away and overextended I tumbled to the floor, my breath rushing out as I hit the earth. I whipped the knife around, but he was gone in that instant, back through the archway.

The tunnel turned black.

I listened to Sam's screams for help, his fleeting footsteps echoing down the corridor as he sprinted away. Pursuit? No, he had too much of a lead. Cursing, I scooped up his bag, retreated deeper into the catacombs.

Pulse pounding, panting breaths echoing all around me, I struggled to think, to grasp this turn of events. What would Sam do when he reached the surface? He would seek help from the priests, from the police. Yes, but it would be difficult to make himself understood, to find someone who knew English.

I had time. I'd flee into the lower tunnels; find an exit far from the cathedral.

But I made a foolish error. In my haste and panic, I'd forgotten to retrieve my candle. I knew it impossible to go back. If Sam's calls had already been heard...

Instead, I sped into the inky depths of the Earth, cradling the bag in one arm, my free hand extended out to deflect any unseen wall or overhang. In this absolute darkness, I missed the turns I knew, blindly ricocheted from wall to wall, and lost all perception of direction. When calmness at last reached me, I spent hours in systematic attempts to map my progress through the maze, but I only became more and more hopelessly lost.

Hours passed, perhaps days. It was impossible to know. I grew tired and hungry. The air was desert dry and a horrible thirst overtook me. By chance my opened palm came across a damp spot in the wall. I hoped it touched some underground stream. Picking at the rock with my knife, I carved out a finger-length trough to collect moisture, even pressed my mouth to the stone and tried to suck water from the earth. I split my teeth on that rock, and earned not even a drop. Useless. I moved on, thirst unabated.

Three times I slept in these passages, haunting the bowels of the Earth like the damned in Hades. "This will be your tomb," a voice said. But I drove it away.

At last there was a hope. My groping fingers came across two familiar indentions on the wall, my initials! The long, straight first letter, the second curved, I had found the spot where I'd carved them after my first robbery, my self-made marker for the exit, a safeguard for lightless passage. Circles! I had walked in circles all this time, never journeying far from the entrance. The cathedral yard was near.

Relief washed over me, the voices slowed. I would soon be free. A close call, but I had kept my reason in the maze and survived. If Sam had missed his ship, I might have revenge. Yes, revenge...

Yet, all was not as it had been in this familiar passage, the very corridor where I'd dumped the bodies of previous crimes. My searching hands found no remains; no skeletons, no tattered clothes left in the abyss. Gone. Unless the dead walk, someone had cleared them away.

The children's search party? Sam's police? Who else could it be?

I crept cautiously towards my escape.

At last, I reached the low archway where I'd assaulted Sam. I gripped the welcome stone edge, but my fingers pressed on a texture of wood beyond. The exit was sealed, a thick door fastened snugly across it.

No...

I pounded on this obstruction, kicked it, threw the bag harmlessly against its pane. How? How could it be sealed? There wasn't time...

I pressed rough fingers to my temple, tried to recall the date of the notice, the one the priest had torn away. What had it said? What were the priest's words? Or was it Sam? Sam and his avenging police, accelerating the sealing? Yes...Enough of the catacombs for the governor, he would solve the problem forever. Seal it tight as a drum.

I pummeled the door, battered it until my fists were bloodied and raw, then collapsed to the floor, lay there for uncounted time. On the ground were bits of wax, the fashioners of this barrier having burnt candles during its construction. Starving, I devoured the remnants of the wax, even ate pebbles to fool my stomach. With my knife, I scraped at the base of the door, cut away until the blade snapped in my hand. Yet, the door remained steadfast, scarred but little diminished by my efforts.

At last, there were voices. *New voices*. A rescue party? I would face the gallows for a scrap of food, a single drop of water. No... their words were too pretty, too harmonious. My heart sank. It was only that damnable distant choir, their hymns so faint and far away I knew my calls would never be answered. I sobbed in despair, my cries unheard by man or God.

Two days at the door I lay. I learned to judge time by their performances. I had never experienced such hunger, yet, it was the thirst that would finish me. My tongue sat fat and immobile in my mouth, my lips swollen, saliva as thick as pudding, I could scarcely swallow.

Sitting in endless solitude, I tried to distract myself from my coming doom. I dug deep into Sam's bag, discarding clothes, letters, a matchbox. At the bottom, I gripped something hard and rectangular bound in leather. I imagined it his billfold, and though it wouldn't bring salvation, there was a bittersweet satisfaction in having taken it from him. Perhaps he would be stranded in Russia, moneyless as I had been. But it was only Sam's notebook. I cast it aside, felt my strength ebbing, collapsed forward onto my belly, hoarse breaths rising from my throat. This was the end. I was fading into a sleep from which I would never wake.

But I wouldn't die face down like a beggar. I rallied, rolled myself over, shoved the bag under my head, tried to reach comfort in my last moments.

I found only injustice.

Wasn't I Montresor, oh, Providence? I raged. *Wasn't I meant to leave the tunnels unharmed and triumphant?* Sam had switched it. Instead, of his perishing here, it would be I who would rot into...

A palsy took my hands. I pressed them to stillness against the floor, my fingers touching on a lost strip of wax melted into a crevice. A portion of wick remained.

It seemed an answer.

With one of Sam's last matches, I lit the wick, pulled his notebook near. With shaking fingers I turned the pages, vowing to know the mind of my murderer.

The book was filled with the routine observations of a travel journalist, simple sketches of foreign cultures, a few caricatures of politicians and pilgrims; tucked inside was a photograph of a pretty young woman, and towards the back, the outline for a novel: a nostalgic book about a boy in Missouri, his friend, his sweetheart, and a murderer entombed forever in the caverns named Injun Joe.

✗

A FRESH START

by Janice Law

Alvin loved the casino; it raised his spirits the minute he reached the parking lot with the lights of the gambling buses and hotel towers against the dark woods. Inside, glowing rows of slots rose like the cells of a giant hive above the florid red carpeting, a world away from everyday boredom and aggravation and trouble. He always bought a handful of tokens and played a few machines just in case Lady Luck was looking his way. You never knew when you'd hear the welcome rattle of a big payoff, and couldn't it be tonight? Sure it could.

Then off to the tables. Tonight Alvin felt lucky in spite of the fact that the slots had gargled his tokens and produced squat—two dollars to be exact. No use when what he needed was a stake for a serious poker game. Alvin knew that if he could get his hands on a few thousand, he could parlay the cash to a big win. He knew he could. And then he'd have Sammy off his back and his debts settled.

He would still be in the red to the business, but Alvin chose not to think that far out. As long as Megan didn't know about certain discrepancies, he was in the clear, and it was just a matter of time before he could repay himself—and Megan, who owned one half of Rosewood Flooring & Carpet. But didn't he do the real work of laying the flooring and selecting the carpets?

Megan handled the customers, took the orders, and kept the shop front in order. Fortunately, he did the books, though lately she'd been making noises about handling the finances herself. She'd had a course at the community college, a pernicious institution in Alvin's estimation, and she was beginning to show a real interest in double entry and accounts payable.

Alvin eyeballed the floor to see if he could spot a sympathetic face, someone who would loan him a few hundred—even a few hundred would help. Thinking about Megan and the books made him feel uneasy and began to bring down the confidence he had felt in the slot parlor. Get to a table, that's the thing, he told himself. Maybe start with a few hands of blackjack, because being lucky tonight, he'd be lucky there, too. Sure he would.

Stick to the cards; Alvin told himself that regularly. He was a pretty good poker player when he had a real stake, but he hated to waste his time on the casual tables. He needed big time action to bring up the pressure of his life in a positive way, to flip the switch and turn on his personal spotlight. That's how he felt at the tables with a big pile of chips and a serious pot on the line.

The problem was that he couldn't run Rosewood Flooring & Carpet and be at the casino, too. Back in the real world, life flattened out and smelled of formaldehyde and construction glue and was studded with housewives who whined and whose husbands delayed his checks. After a busy day of laying sheet goods and wall-to-wall broadloom, he would find himself on the phone with Sammy, dithering about the over-under for the Knicks game and deciding whether the Heat could beat the spread.

Alvin thought of his sports bets as essential therapy, a little something for his mental health. Like some guys need extra sun in the winter, right? He needed a little excitement, and a bet on a game (not terribly interesting otherwise) was better than Prozac. Why support some pharmaceutical giant when you could deal with Sammy and have a lot of fun? It was a no-brainer.

Or at least it had been. But don't think about losses and ham-handed shooters and defensive dogs, because tonight he was lucky. He had a run at the blackjack table and when he doubled down on his last bet, Alvin walked away with five hundred dollars. Could have stayed, the Lady was with him, but he needed big money fast, and he headed for the poker rooms. Just keep cool, he told himself, grow the stake, and things will be fine.

In this euphoric mood, Alvin began mentally paying off his debts: ten grand to Sammy—though the bookie would maybe take five and let the rest ride. He knew Alvin was good for it. And fifteen, maybe fifteen, he could put back in the business. Wouldn't be the whole debt paid, but, hell, he was paying himself, wasn't he? Making a start was the key thing. And he would. As soon as he got to the table and got some good hands and kept the luck going.

That's what he told Sammy when he saw him leaning against the wall, right outside the partition that separated the serious poker tables from the realm of small bettors. The bookie was not a welcome sight, and Alvin had an impulse to slope off to the roulette tables, even though the house had itself covered every which way on the wheels.

"Alvin." Sammy's voice was hoarse, his vocal chords tobacco cured. His face was smoke cured as well, dark as a Virginia ham, thin and bony with bags under his eyes and lines over his cheeks. His stiff black hair was brushed straight back and beginning to gray. He weighed in the neighborhood of 135 pounds, and there was nothing fearsome about him except for his expressionless black eyes and his heavy mob connections.

"Sammy, my man!" Even Alvin could feel his bonhomie was forced.

"We need to talk," said Sammy. "I need from you a timetable. For certain debts." He had a way of pausing between words, of adding weight to every syllable so that the consequences of an unwise flutter on a Wizards-Bucks over-under came out sounding like the national deficit.

"You see me working on it," Alvin said, stepping confidently toward the doorway.

Sammy blocked the way. Alvin could have moved him with one good push, but that wasn't to be thought of; Sammy came with backup.

"I'd have it faster if you were to advance me—not much, not much," he added, seeing Sammy's expression, "a couple thousand's all, just to get me into one of the better games. I'm lucky tonight—even at blackjack and you know that's not my game."

"This is Friday. Sunday you pay me in full or you expect a visit. Got that?"

"Sure thing," Alvin said. "Reason I'm here."

"Reason you're here is to lose your shirt," said Sammy, and he added a few other things that set up bad vibes all round, deflating the good casino feelings and threatening to drive away Alvin's luck. It was almost as if Sammy didn't want to be paid, Alvin thought. He had to spend several minutes calming his breathing before he could get himself into a game with a decent hand and every prospect of a good night.

✗　　✗　　✗　　✗

Soon, he was doing well, really well, in fact, with chips enough to cash in and pay off Sammy. Alvin was pleased about that. Then he thought that he could raise the bet and maybe—not maybe, certainly—clear up what he'd borrowed from the firm, too. He knew enough bookkeeping to confuse Megan. "Late payments," he'd tell her. Put in a big order, slide the money in somehow. Maybe tell her he'd returned some stuff. There were ways.

He threw his chips into the pot. Every one. And lost on the next hand to a full house. The descent from euphoria to despair was so rapid that Alvin had trouble processing the information. He laid his cards down, pushed his chair back, and stood up. He walked to the outer room like a zombie, past tables playing for five-dollar bets, and on to the slot parlors. Physically he hardly knew where he was; metaphysically, he recognized that he was in deep trouble and sinking further. Rosewood Flooring & Carpet was his only possible hope, but there was no way he'd be able to get cash out on the weekend. That meant trouble with Megan, a confession, even.

Alvin was standing in the middle of the slot parlor with tokens rattling and machines beeping and hooting around him, when he heard a groan. He thought at first that he had voiced his trouble and anguish. Then there was a scream, followed by a sudden shift in the light and the sound of wood and metal parting from cement. The glass walled gallery above listed toward the floor and, with a horrifying thud, a cloud of dust, and an explosion of sparks, the whole construction settled on top of the high stakes poker rooms and plunged the casino floor into darkness and terror.

Alvin had a moment of disbelief and shock before his whole mental system re-calibrated for escape. In clouds of smoke and dust, he pushed his way past the slot players, stunned at their machines or scrambling out of their chairs, shouting for lights and wailing about lost purses and canes. He lunged across the floor, tripping over the fallen and kicking out at debris. A metal walker upended him, and he fell to the carpet in danger of being trampled before he clawed himself upright in the smoky confusion. Some of the disoriented players had panicked, but Alvin knew the casino; he had spent so much time there that he could have found his way blindfolded. Which was about the situation now.

He knew that he had to reach the stairs. To do that, he had to pass under the other gallery. Which had to be still intact, because he, Alvin, lucky tonight, had to reach the stairs, the exits, safety. Though a distant amplified voice pleaded for calm, he fought his way forward, knocking people aside, pushing and kicking until he felt, felt rather than saw, the partition between the slot parlor and the corridor.

Somewhere ahead was the faint red glow of an exit light; behind him, a newly sinister redness and hot fire breath. People were running beside him, the fit and agile making a charge for the wide stairs up to air and night and lights. Alvin got knocked into the wall and bashed his knee against one of the casino's big wooden sculptures.

Why the hell they'd needed artwork in the first place and why they'd laid out enough cash to bribe every artist in the state in the second place were twin mysteries Alvin had sometimes pondered. But not now, because he was lucky, indeed, and while the mob rushed forward he found himself squashed against what he could feel was a door. He guessed that it was one of the private casino doors labeled, *Employees Only*.

He felt for the handle and thrust it open. Sure enough, an alarm shrieked though just about every light in the place was out and every circuit was useless or worse, with broken wires throwing blue and white sparks around the rooms and setting carpeting on fire. Struggling for breath, Alvin stumbled into a hallway. It was pitch dark, but there seemed less smoke and certainly less confusion. He groped forward until his ankle connected with a stair riser. He felt for the banister and started up, one landing, two.

It grew hot as he climbed the stairs, and the smoke that made his eyes water and set him coughing seemed to be increasing. Where was it coming from? But there would be a door at the top, an unlocked door out to the parking lot. And if Alvin were truly lucky, Sammy and his gambling debts would all be buried under several tons of cement and glass and light fixtures and casino décor and burned up like a cancelled betting slip.

Alvin thought that he was near the top, when he stumbled on something, lost his balance, and, in a terrifying skid, bumped down to the landing below. He crawled back up, one hand extended to feel his way. Touched something, make that someone. "Get up," Alvin said. "Get up. We have to get the door open."

No response. Alvin levered himself upright with the banister and stepped over the man, he was pretty sure it was a man; he thought he'd touched a tailored jacket. He flailed around in the darkness, frightened that he'd miss the door or get turned around and tumble down the steps. It would be a bad move to fall, to break a leg or get knocked out, for the stairwell was definitely getting hotter and smokier.

Don't, thought Alvin, *don't think of it. This is my lucky night. Don't panic.* He ran his hands along the wall until he touched, finally, a metal doorjamb with the door push bar to the left. He heard the shriek of the alarm, saw the lights of the parking lot beyond and felt the rush of cold night air offering salvation. "Come on," he called back to the prone figure. "We've got to get out."

No reply. Alvin's first impulse was to run, but with the discovery of the door and the certainty of escape, his panic receded. His better nature sent him back to kneel beside the figure, where he forced himself to pat the shoulder, to lay his hand against the chest, and touch the neck. No thumping heart, no fluttering pulse. Nothing.

Heart attack possibly. Or stroke. There was no time for a better diagnosis, for heat was coming up the stair well, and who knew what would happen or what sort of pipes were running along the ceiling. Alvin decided to drag the body outside just in case he was wrong, in case the man was breathing. He was struggling to get a grip on his heavy and repulsive burden when he touched something square and firm. It was a wallet, and Alvin could feel that it held a good deal more than his own.

The guy wouldn't need it now, Alvin thought, and he stuck the wallet in his pocket. A little financial reinforcement sure wouldn't come amiss when he didn't even have enough to buy a cup of coffee. Besides, he was owed something, wasn't he, for trying to help?

Alvin opened the door, and, in the faint light from the lots beyond, he looked at the man. Medium height, a bit heavier than he needed to be, with a square face and dark hair rather like Alvin's own. There was Lady Luck for you. Guy with a good job at a casino cops it on the exit stair five feet from safety, while Alvin, who's lost everything, walks out the door.

It could have been me, he thought; instantly, another possibility opened up. Alvin weighed his own wallet and keys. Was he lucky tonight or what? He decided he was, and after the briefest hesitation, he stuck the keys and the wallet into the stranger's pocket and fished up a set of car keys in exchange. With the alarm shrieking in his ears, Alvin stepped out to the parking lot.

Lights, sirens, and screaming emergency vehicles; thick clouds of red tinged smoke against the pinky night sky; hoses and pump trucks, firemen armed with respirators and heavy slickers and boots; cops with their fluorescent vests and bull horns, and drifts of survivors, some already draped in blankets. They would be lined up and organized and identified and kept waiting in some central location.

But he had found an alternate route and could walk out and be gone. For good if he wanted, leaving behind Sammy and Megan and Rosewood Flooring & Carpet and the threat of visits from collection agencies, legit and otherwise. Alvin felt the euphoria of the evening returning: this was his biggest gamble yet.

He just needed to find the car. Guessing that the man was an employee and that his car would be parked nearby, Alvin walked to the nearest lot and began tapping the key. Five minutes later, he saw lights go on in a big Cadillac. He had his ride and a nice one it was, too, with leather seats and a fancy dashboard with a GPS screen.

Alvin got in and backed the car out of its parking slot. He left the lights off and negotiated by the stanchions still glowing against the smoke filled sky. He drove to the far end of the lot, shut his motor off, and waited with his head down until a brace of police vehicles raced past him, then pointed the Caddie to the exit road and the state highway.

The reaction set in a few miles along the winding country road when he started shaking and turned cold and thought he would lose everything he'd ever eaten. Alvin pulled over and sat with the car door open and his head between his legs, while waves of nausea surfed on images of the collapsing gallery and the black stairwell and the screams of the gamblers whose luck had run out for good. *I could be dead*, Alvin thought. *I could be squashed flat as road kill and just as dead.*

When he could finally get back behind the wheel, he pushed the heater up to full power and eased back onto the state road, trembling all over and driving like an invalid. A lighted donut shop promised warmth and food; he pulled into the lot and checked the wallet.

When he saw the dense pack of hundred dollar bills, Alvin started to laugh. If there was nothing smaller, he still wouldn't be able to get coffee, and he'd be no better off than when he left the poker table. Alvin took several minutes to regain control, then further investigation revealed a twenty and two singles, courtesy of Matthew P. Newthorpe, who stared back at him from his laminated driver's license. It gave Alvin an odd feeling to see that Matt, who was dead and now reborn, was less than a year older and the same height to the inch.

Alvin went into the shop and ordered a cup of coffee and a sugar donut.

"To go?" the girl asked. She was a washed out blonde with an over bite and dark patches under her eyes, who looked too young to be working so late.

"I'll have it here," Alvin said, for he realized suddenly that he had no place to go. He sat down at one of the plastic tables and warmed his hands on his coffee cup, then dunked the donut in the hot liquid and tried to bring various bodily systems back on line.

He had a strong impulse to tell the counter girl about the casino disaster, the collapsing gallery, the darkness and smoke, about what it felt like to step on other human beings and how he, himself, had nearly been trampled. Alvin recognized that thought as a potentially bad move. He refilled his cup and bought another donut, instead.

The shop was warm and bright. Alvin felt that he had had enough darkness to do him for quite some time, and he would like to have spent the rest of the night eating donuts and telling the counter girl about his adventures. *Don't do it*, he thought, although Alvin realized that it wasn't natural to escape from such a horror and say nothing.

And don't stay too long, either, for off in the distance, he heard the wail of an ambulance. Some emergency vehicles might come this way. Or the cops would and wouldn't they stop for coffee, donuts, a chat with the counter girl? Alvin got up. He was tempted to leave her a big tip but that would not do. Matthew P. Newthorpe could not afford to draw attention to himself.

He nodded and went out. When the cold night air hit him, he began to shiver again with delayed shock. Alvin decided that he had to find somewhere warm. He could hardly drive to the Newthorpe residence and let himself in, even though he had the keys. There could be a Mrs. Newthorpe, maybe small Newthorpes with their father's dark hair and weak eyes, even a white-haired mom or dad.

Alvin reminded himself that he had to fight fantasy and keep control. Matt Newthorpe was no more unless you counted Alvin himself, who would soon disappear and turn Newthorpe's cash into a fresh start. He had to focus on that and on luck, on the idea that this was his lucky night.

Just the same it was hard to concentrate when he could still hear screams and groans, human and material, and when good fortune and calamity kept jostling each other for priority. He was feeling very tired, too, and Alvin decided that he'd take a room. He'd get a good sleep and make a fresh start in the morning. He repeated that to himself several times as he started the car and turned it around and headed for the interstate where he knew there were motels.

He was so concentrated on his plans that he did not notice the dark car at the back of the lot. The driver pulled out without lights a few seconds later and tracked him down the interstate to a big chain motel. Alvin went in, obtained a room, and came out to move his car to the far side of the building. The dark car followed, and when Alvin parked the Cadillac, stopped directly behind.

Alvin got out and turned, curious. It was his lucky night and he did not feel uneasy, only vaguely puzzled, until a man stepped from the car and pointed a gun at him. "Hey," said Alvin. "What's the matter?"

"You know what's the matter, Newthorpe."

Alvin tried to explain; he fished up the wallet and pointed to the glasses on the real Matthew P. Newthorpe. "If it's the money," he said, fumbling for the bills, but that was either a mistake or too late, because there was a sharp, popping sound. Alvin was flung back against the Caddie's shiny flanks, and he was still trying to explain about Lady Luck and fresh starts and the vast differences between himself and Matthew P. Newthorpe, when he slid off the fender and dropped, silent, to the ground.

✗

THE RUBA ROMBIC ROBBERIES

by Gary Lovisi

A BENTLEY HOLLOW COLLECTABLES MYSTERY

"**M**r. Hollow," the voice over the telephone pleaded. "My name is John Castle and I'm calling because my wife and I are very worried about our Ruba Rombic."

"Ruba…who?"

"Rombic! Ruba Rombic!" the man at the other end of the line said intently. "It's not a 'who', it's a 'what'. Ever hear of it?"

"Okay, Ruba…What?" I replied, confusion and annoyance creeping into my voice as I wondered just what this fellow wanted. Since my wife had left me and I'd retired from the police, I'd led a rather quiet life these days, buying and selling antique collectable glassware, playing a little golf, buying some old books.

"Ruba Rombic, it's Depression Glass," he explained.

"Oh," I replied with a shrug. Though I collected Depression Glass, I'd never heard of this variety.

"Mr. Hollow, I read about you in the local paper last year, that thing about the Fenton Art Glass and the old lady who died."

"Yes," I replied carefully.

"So I thought I'd call to hire you. Our Ruba Rombic has been stolen and my wife and I are at our wits' end. We want you to get it back for us."

"Ah, look, Mr…?"

"Castle, John Castle. My wife's name is Susan."

"Well, Mr. Castle, I'm retired now. I don't even know what this Ruba Rombic is and even if I did, I'm not a licensed private investigator. You need to go to the police if you have been the victim of a robbery."

"I know that, but you're a collector," Castle said seriously. "That's what matters most."

So that's how I got into it. The next day I drove out to Wood-mere and the nice big house that John and Susan Castle lived in. The Castles' castle.

He was a retired industrialist and she did volunteer work and collected antiques. They seemed like nice people. They were both big art deco collectors, which was a bit out of my area of interest and affordability. I collected Depression Era glassware—but I soon discovered the two areas did overlap—they overlapped especially when it came to Ruba Rombic.

I shook my head as I looked at the photos Mrs. Castle showed me of the precious glassware items she said had been stolen from their home.

"Aren't they lovely!" she gushed.

Could she be serious? I kept mum. It certainly appeared to be some kind of glassware, Depression Era for sure, but I'd never seen the likes before. I'll give them this, the stuff was certainly unique—there was nothing quite like it in Depression glass. I learned later that it was made from 1928 to 1932 by the Consoli-dated Lamp and Glass Company—designed by Ruben Haley—but the main thing about it to me was that it was so damn incredibly ugly. I mean, it looked like something created by a mad man's warped brain, or a bad Flintstones episode. It looked like it was glassware straight from Wilma and Fred's dinner table.

"Aren't they beautiful?" Susan Castle added. "The Cubist-in-spired geometric forms make it one of the most original American glass designs of the 20th century. It's the essence of Art Deco/Art Moderne."

I flipped through the photos again without comment, because I hardly knew what to say. The stuff was absolutely horrid. It was unbelievably gross and though I collected Depression Glass and loved it all because it was so lovely and esthetically pleasing, this stuff was quite different. The photos showed me items that were apparently pitchers, cups, plates, bowls, and vases, all of various colors of glass, but hardly your garden variety, nicely-done De-pression Glass. This stuff was composed of hard geometric shapes with harsh sharp angles that made each piece look twisted and bi-zarre. It was atrocious stuff.

I stared at each photo with astonishment and dismay, while the Castles' spouted amazing monetary figures for the values of each piece. Five thousand, ten thousand, twenty thousand dollars for certain pieces. That the stuff was rare I could well believe, but that it was worth so much money seemed incredible.

"They're simple, yet so quintessentially Art Deco," John Castle enthused. "Rombic means irregular in shape with no parallel lines. Ruba came from Rubaiy, meaning an epic poem, or perhaps it was a shortening of the designer, Ruben Haley's first name. No one knows for sure. It's not important. What is important is that our collection is gone and we want it back."

"John and I bought each piece many years ago, Mr. Hollow," Susan Castle added sadly.

"You can call me Ben, short for Bentley," I said.

"Thank you, Mr. Hollow," she replied, ignoring my request. I could see she was devastated by the loss. She went on, "We bought our pieces decades ago when there was no market to speak of, we paid very little. It was a steal, really. Since then, however, advanced Art Deco collectors and even museums have started displaying Ruba Rombic. Prices have shot up astronomically."

"Our problem, Mr. Hollow," John Castle explained, "is that we could never replace this collection if it were lost to us forever. It's not a matter of insurance money, it's that you cannot find the pieces anywhere. Period."

"So they're scarce?" I asked.

"Rare, Mr. Hollow. They are rare, none are to be found," Castle replied. "It is estimated less than 1,500 pieces have survived."

"So why me? Why not go to the police?"

John Castle nodded, "Good question. We did go to the police, of course, initially. They told us…"

"Mr. Hollow," Susan Castle interrupted, "we know who took the pieces. It was Simon James, another collector."

My eyebrows arched. I'd heard the name, of course. James was a mover and shaker in our fair city.

"And you told this to the police?" I asked.

"Of course, but nothing was ever found in a search of James' home. James is a collector too, and has a wonderful grouping of pieces, among them a top-notch collection of Ruba Rombic, but of course all his pieces are validated with bills of sale from reputable dealers. He showed these to the detectives with obvious amusement. The police found nothing incriminating."

"The bottom line, Mr. Hollow, is that our complaint, without any proof, means the police will not investigate any further. Captain Wallace told us he could not afford to bother such an important member of the community without conclusive proof," Susan Castle said softly.

"Well, if what you say is true," I said, "he had to have a pro do the actual job. Someone from out of town, I'd guess. Tough to find. A man like James wouldn't steal it himself. But what makes you think a big shot like Simon James would do such a thing? And what would he do with this stuff once he had it? It's not the kind of thing he could easily sell. Even on the collector market, glassware like this would have a very limited interest. The other thing is, if James has a similar collection, why would he even want to steal yours? I mean, it doesn't make sense to me. And you say nothing else was stolen?"

"No, nothing else was touched, only our Ruba Rombic," John Castle admitted.

"I know that son-of-a-bitch stole my precious glass to…Well, you know what he's going to do with it, John? My God, I can't even say it!" Tears rolled down her cheeks. Susan Castle's anger and hopelessness finally had gotten the better of her.

"Easy, Susan," her husband said, comforting his wife with an affectionate hug. "Why don't you go inside and lie down a while. I know you're upset. Take a pill and a nap. I'll square things with Mr. Hollow."

Susan Castle dried her tears. "Get them back for me, Mr. Hollow, please."

I watched as she walked into a bedroom down the hall. She shut the door behind her with a loud slam. I was left alone with her husband.

"My wife—she's emotional," John Castle explained.

"I understand, but I don't know if I can help you. Honestly, this all sounds very confusing. Why would someone like Simon James steal this stuff?"

Castle sighed, "He's a collector too, Mr. Hollow. He and I have the largest collections of Ruba Rombic in the world. You see, Simon and I go way back. We began in business and politics decades ago, we also began buying up Depression glassware when it was dirt cheap—especially Ruba Rombic. Now each piece is going for big money."

"Okay, I understand that," I said, my eyes darting to the photos of the missing glassware. I shook my head, wondering who would even want to collect this stuff. I figured the only reason it must be so valuable today is that when it was sold in the 1930s no one had bought it. I sighed. "Look, what could a big-shot like Simon James do with the stuff? He could never sell it."

"Mr. Hollow, my wife and I know Simon James well. He doesn't want to add our pieces to his collection. He doesn't even want to sell them for money. What Simon James wants to do with our Ruba Rombic collection—is destroy it. He will break each piece into tiny shards of useless glass. That is what is disturbing my wife so much."

"But why destroy it?" I asked amazed.

"So that he will have the best collection of Ruba Rombic in the world and so that his collection will increase substantially in value," Castle said matter-of-factly.

I laughed. That certainly seemed twisted, but being a collector myself, I knew the collector mentality. Any collector worth his salt would never even consider such a thing, but a few—certain ones— well, they just might. Castle's words were not as far from the realm of possibility as they sounded.

"And you and your wife actually believe this?"

"Years ago when we were on social terms, Simon even told us as much when he first saw our collection. He lamented how, without the existence of our pieces, his own collection would become the finest in the entire world. He told me with a smile then how the value of his pieces would easily quadruple in value."

I nodded. The dark side of the collector mentality.

"We can pay you well, Mr. Hollow," John Castle continued, handing me a small piece of paper which I looked at, noting a substantial number followed by four zeroes. I gladly placed the check in my pocket. Castle added, "Can you look into it? See what you can find out? Please."

"I'll look into it," I said carefully, "but I can't promise much if the police have come up empty. Any idea where James would stash the stolen goods?"

"No," Castle said helplessly. "The police didn't find anything incriminating at his home."

"What about his destruction of the glass?" I asked. "It's been a few weeks, it may be gone by now."

Castle shook his head nervously. "I hope not. I don't think so. He'd want to look each piece over, savor each item for a while before he destroys them. At least that's what I've told Susan, to calm her—she gets so worried that the glass may have already been destroyed."

"And you don't think so?" I asked.

"No. Not yet. I don't think so."

"I think you may be right, Mr. Castle," I said, thinking of what I knew of the collector mentality—but I also knew I didn't have much time. I had a lot of work to do. I got ready to leave. "I'll be in touch, Mr. Castle."

John Castle's check would be a boon to my police pension and allow a bit left over to buy a Depression Glass piece I'd had my eye on in an Internet auction. Since my wife, Beth, had left me for a doctor last year, I'd been living alone in an empty house with only the glassware she had left behind for company. I missed the wife but at least I had the glassware. That Depression Glass is really quite lovely; bright, colorful, graceful even, with so many charming patterns—but this Ruba Rombic stuff…sheesh! I hadn't wanted to mention to the Castles that I thought the stuff was brutal. I mean, if my glass collection was made of vomit, I'd have Ruba Rombic too! Still and all, this was a paying case and I'd been given a nice-size check to do the job as best I could.

My first step was to call my friend Detective Jackie Harris to get the lowdown on just what the police file had on the robbery; also to get her take on the Castles and Simon James.

"Ben," Jackie told me over the phone, "a search warrant was issued and came up blank on the house on Michigan Avenue. As far as the robbery, it looked legit, but it's a dead end. No prints, the alarm was circumvented. The Castles were out of town at the time. Only that damn glassware was missing. It was a pro job for sure, or an inside job."

"Inside job?" I asked quickly. "What makes you say that?"

"Well, maybe. The husband and wife don't always seem to get along. There seems to be some tension there. That glass is supposed to be worth a small fortune, pretty amazing, eh? Anyway, my partner thinks that maybe one of them stole it, to hide it from the other?"

"Any evidence of that?" I asked.

"No," she replied carefully. Did she know more than she was willing to tell me? I wondered. Usually Jackie was very up front, but now that I was retired and out of the loop, she might be holding back a card or two.

"I don't know," I said thoughtfully. "That doesn't make sense to me, from what I've just seen of them. They hired me together to find the stuff, they're both adamant that James stole it—or hired someone to steal it. And they do seem to get along well enough, your average retired older couple. I didn't see any tension between the two."

"Oh well, that's all we have now. Nothing on the street about the break-in, or anything about any valuable glassware. We squeezed the usual fences and informants. Checked the local pawn shops. Nada."

"What about Simon James?" I asked.

Jackie was silent for a moment, "That's a bit complicated."

"What do you mean?" I told Jackie the Castles' theory of why James had stolen their glassware.

"Yeah, I remember them telling us something like that. Seems crazy but I could see James being like that, you know, that kind of person. If he can't have it—no one else can," Jackie said, then added, "But, Ben, we've got nothing on him and he's got a lot of juice in this town. Captain Wallace was told to back off unless he had substantial and serious proof. Being Captain Wallace…well, you know."

"Yeah, thanks, Jackie."

Jackie's info didn't leave me much to go on. I made a mental note that I'd probably want to speak with Simon James at some point but in the meantime I did an extensive Internet search of the big man and this glassware. Not only Google, but I emailed all my contacts in the collectable glassware field for info. I wanted to know if James bought from them and what he bought. How did he pay? What was he like to deal with?

I came up with a lot of info, most of it seemingly contradictory. Simon James was a big player in the Depression Glassware field, aside from being wealthy and powerful overall. He lived in a big house and collected all kinds of things but seemed to specialize in Art Deco works and Depression Era glassware. His house was filled with it—but it was big enough to hold whatever he wanted. By all accounts he had an extensive and priceless collection. It didn't make sense to me that such a man would cause this theft—unless you were a collector yourself and knew someone who was this type of collector, I kept telling myself.

I smiled. That's why John Castle had been so adamant on my taking this case, and why he knew that being a collector myself I was the right person for the job.

The Internet proved to be a wash. Contacts via email were better but didn't really pan out. James bought a lot of stuff from the same people and places I bought from—just a lot of higher-end items for a lot more money. I was about to call it all off and close up shop on the Castles when I got a call from Jenny Rogers at Kalamazoo Arts.

"Hi, Ben," Jenny said cheerily with her usual enthusiasm. We went back a bit, Beth and I had been buying and selling to her for years. I'd kept up the relationship. "You know, you still owe me $75 for that Peach Lustre bowl."

"Yeah, I remember. I was just going to send you a check," I said. "Don't worry, I didn't forget you."

"I know, Ben. The check is in the mail. I know you're busy and all. Look, I didn't call you to remind you to pay your bill—though that would be nice…"

I laughed, "Sure."

"And you didn't hear this from me, understand?"

"Yes," I said, more attentive now.

"This Simon James; I've never met him but he buys from me a lot, also from some other dealers I know. Well, when you emailed me about what he buys and pays, it's only the best stuff and he pays top dollar. You can understand I don't want to lose him as a customer."

"Sure," I replied. "I've heard all that. His house is full of only the best stuff. It's like a museum."

"Well, that's just it. I ship almost all the stuff to his home on Michigan Avenue, but..."

"Almost? Where's the rest of the stuff go?"

"That's just it, he's got another house."

"Really?" I asked totally interested now.

"Well, it's not really a house, it's some kind of hunting lodge up in the mountains. He's very secretive about it and I always feel like I'm doing something not quite on the up-and-up when he has me ship there..."

I smiled, "Jenny, you're a peach! What's the address?"

I drove up right away. The house was in the mountains outside of town. It was not exactly a hunting lodge and not exactly a mansion. I left my car on the side of the highway and walked up the icy road. The house was set back in the snowy woods, alone, quiet. It looked like it was closed for the winter. I wondered.

The place was a two floor log home with a pointed roof and a wooden porch all around it. The lights were off. It looked deserted. I carefully walked up the pathway, onto the porch and found a doorbell. I rang it.

There was no answer.

I rang it again and again.

No answer again.

Now I had to decide, bite the bullet, earn my money for the Castles or give it up and slink away, never to know the truth. I took a deep breath. B&E wasn't my usual thing but there were questions I wanted answered and besides, I needed the money. I used my shoulder to break in the front door. It wasn't a very solid door and after three tries it flew open and I flew inside.

The place was dark, but there was enough daylight left for me to look around. What I found was an amazing accumulation of boxes—Postal Service, UPS, FedEx. Some opened, others still sealed. They were piled throughout every room; the place was overrun with various collectables. Especially glassware—Depression Era glassware. I walked around, marveling at all the lovely objects, some things I knew I could never afford and would never own. I was amazed as I walked through room after room.

I found the Castles' Ruba Rombic collection on the kitchen table. All the missing pieces were there, wrapped up in boxes. Now what to do?

I thought of calling the cops of course; making Simon James pay for his crime and even more so to me, his violation of the collector's code—stealing from a fellow collector. But it just didn't seem to make sense to get the cops involved and have them over-complicate everything. The cops would make a mess of it, asking me all kinds of nosy questions, with James eventually getting fancy lawyers involved. Those lawyers would make me the darn criminal. His people would accuse me of B&E, theft, whatever else they could. I knew that wouldn't end well for me.

Or I could just put the stuff in my car and drive over to the Castles and give it back to them. Which is just what I did.

I carried the boxes into the house carefully, one at a time from the back of my car. The Castles were shocked and overjoyed when they looked at what was in those boxes.

"You found them!" Susan Castle cried in joy, suddenly planting a kiss on my cheek. She called her husband and they looked through each box in sheer delight.

"Mr. Hollow, you are amazing," John Castle said obviously relieved. I placed the boxes on the dining room table and both husband and wife got busy going through each box, carefully unwrapping their precious objects, looking them over minutely, then lovingly placing them inside a large oak display case.

"John, they're home," Susan Castle said in relief. She delicately placed the last piece of that infernally ugly Ruba Rombic into the display case and locked the glass door with a small key.

I smiled, "I guess it's an acquired taste."

"You either love 'em or you hate 'em," John Castle answered with a knowing smile. "So where did you find them? What did Simon James say when he was arrested?"

I held up my hands. "There's not a lot to say about that. You wanted your precious Ruba Rombic back, so here it is. Safe and sound. The less said about any of this—my involvement, your suspicions about Simon James, or even the fact that you have it back at all—well, it would be best for all concerned to keep mum. You get my drift?"

"Then he gets away with it?" Susan Castle flared in anger.

"He gets away with nothing. Your property is returned to you and without any damage, just as you wanted," I replied more forcefully.

She nodded slowly. I saw her face soften as she looked over at the rescued glassware that now filled her display case. "Well, then thank you, Mr. Hollow…Ben. We won't say another word."

"You did a hell of a job," John Castle added. "My only regret is missing out on seeing the look on Simon James' face when he realizes that the items he filched from us, have been filched from him. There's justice in that, at least. You've made me and my wife very happy. Thank you."

"There's just one more thing, Ben," the wife said rather hesitantly. "This box over here. These six pieces. They are not ours."

"Really? Are you sure?" I asked, watching as John now examined the pieces and soon concurred with his wife.

"Nope, not ours at all," he stated.

"So what now?" I asked.

The Castles looked at me. "Well, they're not ours and we do not want them."

"Well, I can't put them back now," I stammered, perplexed by the problem. "I mean, it was a big risk taking the stuff in the first place."

"Well, why don't you just keep them?" Susan Castle asked.

"Yeah, Mr. Hollow, Simon will miss them but then again, he probably stole them too," John Castle added. "Who knows, maybe you'll be contacted by the true owner and will be able to return them? If not, just look at it as the perks of the job."

"I don't know, it would be too risky to return them now, and I guess I could hold on to them for a while…but that stuff is just… so damn ugly!" I said with a smile. Then I looked at the six pieces in the box more closely. "You know, this stuff does kinda grow on you. I think I'm actually getting to like it. In fact, they might fit well in my own collection if no one claims them. After all, I am a Depression Glass collector and this Ruba Rombic is sorta unique."

✗

ONLY THE DEAD

by Gordon Linzner

Wind tore at Paddy McGuire's threadbare ulster, drove stinging rain into his face, as he hurried across the Great Bridge. He pulled his cap more tightly onto his head and reached again beneath the coat for the cudgel tucked in his belt. Its heft should have been more reassuring.

Electric lights, first on any bridge in the world, made his shadow lengthen and shrink, lengthen and shrink, on the wooden walkway. A dozen years after the bridge opened, connecting two of the country's greatest cities, and Paddy still marveled at that yellow glow.

But not tonight. Never had the sky seemed so dark, the city behind so looming, the choppy waters forty yards below so black and threatening. The boards beneath his feet trembled with the vibration of a passing elevated train. He thrust a hand into his right coat pocket, fingering anew his latest prize. Perhaps it was only the October night's bitter cold, but the metal seem to burn against his flesh.

He glanced back over his shoulder. Up here he could see he was no longer being followed. In the dark, twisting streets near the fish market, footsteps echoed all around, shadows shifted in every corner. That drunken Lascar had not been as alone as Paddy'd thought, though his fellow sailors had not been close enough to save him.

Other footpads in New York's Five Points district mocked Paddy's frequent journeys to Brooklyn. Inefficient and corrupt and loath to cooperate as the police were on both sides of the East River, however, they occasionally captured a felon. By shifting between jurisdictions, Paddy had extended his career long past that of many of his fellows.

A gust of rain blinded him; he wiped his eyes. When he blinked them open again, what he saw made him gasp.

A crowd was racing at him from the Brooklyn side, less than twenty yards away, faces contorted in panic. A woman in the lead slipped and fell, to be trampled by the others. Paddy felt a sharp pain in his ribs, and struggled for a moment to breathe.

Yet, most disturbing, there was no of sound. The woman's cries, the mob's shouts, were apparently lost in the pounding rain and shrill wind.

Paddy leapt to the side of the walkway to pull himself onto one of the cables, out of harm's way. As he reached up, he saw a wheelbarrow, a workman still gripping its handles, plunge off the far tower. What the devil was the man doing up there in this storm? Paddy froze, distracted. His hand slipped on rain-slick steel. He fell backwards onto the walkway.

Now the crowd was almost upon him, though he still could not hear them nor feel the boards tremble under their approach. He covered his head and curled up, presenting as small a target as possible, tensing for the impact of trampling heels.

A minute passed.

Two.

"Are you well, sir?"

Paddy opened one eye. A man wearing a long frock coat, holding a top hat in place with one hand, stood over him. He looked little older than Paddy's own one score year and four, though the stubble on his puffy face indicated a dissipation more common to more senior aristocrats. His other hand clutched a cane with a heavy brass grip Paddy suspected was not entirely decorative.

Paddy slowly unfurled his body and felt beneath the ulster for his cudgel, which dug painfully into his gut. Under other circumstances, on this deserted bridge, the stranger would seem a perfect victim. Paddy was too rattled to consider anything but self-defense.

"The mob," he gasped. "Were you one? Did you see?"

The gentleman tucked the cane beneath his arm, held out a hand. "I only saw you slip and fall."

"The woman! She must be hurt, maybe dead."

The stranger shook his head. "No woman of sense would walk alone in such weather, in isolation."

Paddy sat up, ignoring the outstretched hand. He looked east and west. He was midway between the bridge's towers. The walkway was empty, save for the stranger.

"I, ah, must have been thinking of something that happened earlier." A dozen years earlier, he realized with a shock. A panic on the bridge shortly after its opening had created just the scene he had imagined.

And the workman? One of the crew who died during construction?

Paddy pulled himself to his feet.

"You seem shaken," the other said. "Shall I accompany you? Alone, unsteady on your feet, you may be vulnerable to criminals."

The irony of the man's solicitude was not lost on Paddy. "I'm fine. Just had the wind knocked out by the fall." He bounced on his heels to prove his haleness, and instantly regretted doing so; the motion made his gut roil.

If the gentleman noticed Paddy's discomfort, he gave no sign. "Then, if I can be of no further service, I bid you good night. Perhaps our paths will cross again."

The stranger turned and strode towards the city of Brooklyn.

Paddy gazed over the harbor, giving the gentleman a respectable lead. Despite the lashing rain, he could just make out the silhouette of Fort Columbus on Governors Island, and the illuminated torch of the new colossus, *Liberty Enlightening the World*, now dominating Bedloes Island. North of the statue sat the newly opened wooden immigration station on Ellis Island. Paddy himself had entered America two decades earlier with his parents, through the former Fort Clinton, now being converted to an aquarium.

His parents and baby sister had succumbed to influenza when he was ten. He'd been on his own ever since.

Paddy reached into his pocket again. His prize was secure. The indentations along the four sides of the otherwise smooth gold bar meant nothing to him. They did not need to.

If he glanced right or left, Paddy imagined shapes hurtling past the cables to the East River below. He looked down after the first one, but saw no sign of impact. Thereafter he focused his eyes straight ahead. The weather must be playing tricks on his mind, that was all.

If not for the storm, ferries would be crisscrossing those waters into the small hours of the morning. One of them would have borne the Lascar and his burden long before. Instead, the sailor had been waiting for the storm to ease, whiling his time in a tavern in the bridge's shadow, shedding his inhibitions enough to provide Paddy with motive and opportunity to better his own fortunes.

The thief continued past the Brooklyn tower, descending until he came to ground on Sands Street. At least the maze of factories, warehouses, and tenements provided some respite from the wind. He paused beneath the anchorage. Despite glass casements, many street gas lamps had been extinguished by the wind and rain. Paddy needed no light to tell that his brogans were soaked through. He wrung out his cap and shook himself. This set his body shivering, as if it realized for the first time how thoroughly sodden it was.

Paddy took deep breaths, willing his frame to steady itself. The rain was letting up, and safe haven was only a few blocks away. He fitted his cap back in place. Huge commercial buildings, some over ten stories high, sat silent alongside the bridge like the sarcophagi of giants, but to the north lay a more residential prospect.

Paddy started across Sands Street.

The rumble of an elevated train coming off the Great Bridge almost drowned out the screech of the trolley on its rails. Paddy hurled himself back, heels skittering against slick paving stones.

No passengers were visible in the open-sided vehicle. Most likely it was heading to the yards, and so the driver was more heedless of pedestrians than usual.

Electric street cars had begun running in Brooklyn a few years earlier, and quickly grew prolific. Many Brooklynites chose to dodge around or in front of the vehicles, which moved swifter than the horse-cars preceding them. Not every Trolley Dodger succeeded. Only during the great trolley strike this past January had the streets of Brooklyn felt safe. The number of maimings and fatalities mounted daily.

As if to underline the fact, a boy of perhaps twelve suddenly shot from the shadows directly into the path of the trolley that had just missed Paddy.

The trolley's carriage caught the boy on his side. He spun around once before falling onto the tracks. Paddy winced, grabbing his own arm.

The trolley continued on.

Paddy rushed to where the boy had fallen.

The tracks were empty.

Suppressing a shiver that had nothing to do with rain or cold, Paddy traced the tracks up Sands Street. He found no blood, no body parts, not even a shred of clothing.

He definitely needed of get out of this weather.

Paddy turned west on Duffield Street, which was lined with modest private homes dating back decades. Gaslight flickered in several of the houses; the rest were dark, their inhabitants either abed or too frugal to waste money on the utility.

At one time this area, Vinegar Hill—named for a century-old battle in Ireland—had been well to do, but the construction of the bridge cast a pall over it. Nor was the area likely to recover. There was talk of adding a second and even a third bridge across the waters. The Great Bridge was too popular to handle the traffic load.

The house near the corner of Duffield and York had been built around 1830, shortly after New York State banned slavery. Prior to the Civil War, it, like many of its neighbors, had been a stop on the underground railroad. Brooklyn had been a hot-bed of abolitionist activity. Several tunnels still led from surrounding basements to the docks. Paddy had used one just last year, to avoid a gang that had gotten too interested in some booty he'd been carrying.

Paint peeled off the clapboard façade in long strips; one of the shaded windows boasted a diagonal crack. An iron knocker shaped like a lion's head clung to the front door. Paddy climbed onto the narrow porch, avoiding the less solid-looking boards, and rapped loudly three times.

The wind had died down. The rain was but a drizzle. He heard shuffling from within.

"Open up, Gee! It's Paddy! I've something to show you!"

A faint muttering came from beyond the door, as if the inhabitant was debating with himself. Then the door creaked open.

Neighbors speculated that the elderly Negro known only as Gee might have been among the earliest escapees along the underground railroad, and had decided to settle here rather than move on to Canada. He was certainly old enough.

Gee could neither read nor write, but he could look at a pilfered piece of jewelry and tell its worth within a few dollars. Gee did not buy stolen goods—he rarely had more money about than required for his simple needs—but was not adverse to taking a cut in payment for his appraisal.

Although the house had gas lighting, Gee preferred candlelight. He disliked the smell of gas, he said. A few candles and a clever arrangement of mirrors provided all the light he needed. The smoke also helped to cover the often unpleasant odors from the river.

"Wet," Gee observed. His eyes moved up to look past Paddy. Paddy looked around, saw nothing, shrugged and pushed his way in. Gee sighed, adding his own shrug.

"I wasn't followed," Paddy said. "I lost them an hour ago."

Gee followed his guest to the parlor. He was not talkative at the best of times, and the weather underscored that. Paddy didn't care.

"Wait until you see this." Paddy dumped his dripping ulster in a corner of the sparsely furnished room, pulling his prize from its pocket. He held it concealed in his hand a moment, enjoying yet loathing the dichotomy of cold and heat the object generated. Then he set it gingerly in the middle of the table and stepped back.

The gold ingot was no longer than his palm, and about two fingers thick. Each of its four sides was etched with symbols that were not quite familiar.

The Negro stared at it. He licked his lips. Usually Gee would handle whatever Paddy brought him to evaluate, raise it to his eyes, almost taste it. This time he seemed reluctant even to approach the table.

"You haven't a drop of whiskey about, have you?"

"Rum."

"That'll do."

Gee made no move to serve Paddy. His eyes stayed fixed on the ingot shimmering in the candlelight.

"Ever seen anything like that?" Paddy asked, to break the spell.

"Once."

"What do you think those markings mean?"

"That, of course, is what *I* hope to discover," came another voice. "Good evening, Mr. McGuire. Again."

Paddy swung about, reaching for his cudgel. He found himself facing the gentleman from the bridge, still in his frock coat and top hat, both considerably drier than Paddy's own outerwear. Behind him stood a swarthy man in a red sailor's shirt, holding a Colt pistol aimed at Paddy's heart.

This focused his attention admirably.

"If this is like the other artifacts I've received, and it should be, the hieroglyphs are some strange amalgam of Hebraic, ancient Egyptian, perhaps Sanskrit," the man continued, "but do not translate in any of those tongues. Any translation, moreover, would only scratch the surface of the secrets they contain, secrets of life and death, as I suspect you have discovered for yourself. Of course, I've barely begun my studies. It may take decades to solve their mysteries, and that's *with* the help of my associates." He nodded toward the sailor with the pistol.

Paddy glowered at Gee. "You might have warned me."

Gee looked at, then past, Paddy.

"Oh," Paddy said, chastened.

"Now, Mr. McGuire, would you remove that stick from your waist and drop it in the far corner? My cane has a longer reach, I assure you. More to the point, this fellow would welcome an excuse to try out his new shooting skills."

Paddy relinquished his weapon. "You have the advantage of me," he admitted.

"Robert Suydam is my name. My family came to these shores some two hundred and fifty years before yours. I say this by way of asserting my rights to that object, since you chose to interfere with my courier."

"How did you know? Who I am, where I'd be going, even that I had your property? And so quickly?"

Suydam smiled. He obviously did not do so often. "When you are wealthy and well-connected, Mr. McGuire, there are no secrets. The telegraph is a marvelous invention. And there are other ways of communication which I believe should remain beyond your ken."

Paddy let that lie. If Suydam wanted to keep secrets, perhaps his situation was not so dire. "So. I've delivered something you wanted. Surely compensation is in order."

Suydam eyed him narrowly. "I believe you are in earnest."

Paddy smiled.

"I'm almost inclined to offer you something, at that. If only to insure your silence. Unfortunately, the associates of the man you murdered wish a few words with you. After that, the question of your silence will be moot."

"Need they know?" Paddy's eyes flickered to the sailor.

"They already do. And I must stay on good terms with them, to continue my studies."

Paddy shifted his right arm. "Gee? I'll have that rum now. If Mr. Suydam does not object?"

"A last request? Why not?"

Gee, who'd stood silent this whole time, moved cautiously to a side table. He poured rum from a dark brown bottle into a discolored tin cup and handed it to Paddy. He did not pour one for himself, nor did he offer any to Suydam or the sailor. He did, however, move to a corner, making himself as inconspicuous as possible.

Paddy breathed in the sugary aroma. Pity to waste it. "To great mysteries," he proposed, raising the cup in his left hand.

Suydam nodded slightly.

One moment the rum was at Paddy's lips. The next, it was dashed into the gunman's eyes. The Colt fired at a spot where Paddy no longer stood. A bowie knife slid from under Paddy's right sleeve and lodged in the man's throat.

Suydam raised his cane, then froze. Paddy held the Colt in his right hand and the ingot in his left.

"I've other plans," Paddy said.

"You *are* resourceful," Suydam mused. "Very well, you've earned your courier pay."

"That was then," Paddy replied. "Now I've gone to some extra trouble. Price is going up."

"Name it."

"No. I want you to think it over. Let Gee know when you're ready to negotiate."

"Don't be a fool, Mr. McGuire. You've had a taste of the power of that icon on the bridge. Elsewhere, too. I see it in your eyes. It's dangerous if you don't know what you're doing."

Paddy smiled. He looked at the dead gunman. Above the corpse stood the sailor's doppleganger, gagging at the knife in his throat. For a moment Paddy, too, could not breathe.

"Your point is taken, Mr. Suydam. Don't wait too long. I might decide it's too risky, and drop it off a bridge."

Suydam paled.

Paddy slipped into the hall, opened the front door, then slammed it shut without exiting. He entered the hall closet, felt for the latch in the back, and pulled open a hidden door to the basement. Suydam might have more confederates outside; they would not know about this passage to the river.

Dangerous? This hunk of gold covered with chicken scratches? Suydam had dropped a clue to its nature, and the Lascar's revenant had clinched it. The ingot allowed him to see ghosts, and share their final moments. How many died building the Bridge? Twenty? Thirty? How many died in streetcar accidents every year? Scores?

The sights had been unnerving, but now he knew what they were. The dead can't hurt the living. There was some discomfort as he felt their last moments, but that was tolerable.

Paddy felt his way along the tunnel, following the scent of salt water. Maybe he should hang onto the damned thing. Spiritualists made a fortune with their tricks. How much could a man capable of raising real spirits make?

After several long minutes Paddy saw a glimmer of, not light, but less dark, up ahead. He stopped abruptly. A figure stirred at the edge of the tunnel.

Had he underestimated Suydam? Had Gee betrayed him?

Paddy felt a tightness at his throat, then relaxed. He was looking at an escaping slave, who in his eagerness had slipped in the slime-coated tunnel and broken his neck fifty years or more ago. That was all.

Ahead, a sliver of the starry night was revealed by dispersing clouds. Paddy shivered in the cold air. He should have grabbed his coat. On the other hand, it was so drenched it would have sucked what little heat remained out of his body. No, he'd find something dry nearby.

He came out under an overhang at the edge of the Navy Yard. Surely he could scrounge up a coat or blanket from one of the workers, or a resident across the street. That man slumped against the fence might be persuaded to offer up his coat. Especially with a Colt pistol in his face.

As Paddy drew nearer, he saw the figure's coat was threadbare and of an unfamiliar style. Still, it was better than nothing. The man himself looked unhealthily gaunt.

And hollow-eyed.

And dead.

Paddy felt a gnawing in his stomach.

He turned away, only to face another specter whose skin had been baked red by sun and wind.

Another half turn, and a woman, half-naked, her nose eaten away by disease, closed in on him.

Paddy's own flesh began to burn. Sharp pains shot through his muscles like bullets from a Gatling gun.

These were not ghosts whose passings had been swift, who'd been trampled by a panicking mob or struck by a trolley. These three had suffered lingering deaths, from disease, starvation, exposure. In earlier encounters, Paddy had felt brief pangs, over so quickly they almost did not register. Now long, drawn-out agonies rent his soul.

His knees buckled.

Stand fast, he told himself. There were only three. He could stand the torture long enough to move away.

Then a fourth figure rose out of the East River.

And a fifth.

And row after row beyond them.

He realized who they were now. He'd heard shipyard workers tell stories while he'd hung out in local bars, downing ale and oysters.

The Navy Yard had been built around Wallabout Bay, an inlet where, more than a century earlier, British occupying forces maintained leaking hulls of vessels as prisons for American revolutionaries.

Over eleven thousand men and women died on those ships.

Eleven thousand dead, inflicting their myriad final agonies on Paddy McGuire.

He tried to run. His knees caved. He sank into a heap in the cold mud just outside the Navy Yard, whimpering, shivering, mewling, hand wrapped so tightly about the ingot that the hieroglyphs left a reverse impression on his palm.

Drowned. Starved. Beaten to death. Guts turned inside out by disease. Skin blackened by the sun.

Paddy stuffed his ears with mud, covered his eyes, tried to crawl away. His limbs were too wracked with pain to obey.

The onslaught continued until Paddy McGuire's very thoughts were eaten away to nothing but cowering animal instinct. He mindlessly huddled in filth, rocking back and forth, fingernails torn and bleeding, extremities numb, stinking of his own voided bowels.

Which was how Robert Suydam and three scowling Lascars found him, a few minutes before dawn.

Suydam pried the ingot from Paddy's hand, wrapped it in a handkerchief, and placed it gingerly in his own coat pocket. He turned to the sailors.

"Satisfied?" he asked them.

The three fingered their curved blades, but did not draw them. Killing Paddy McGuire now would be a mercy. They were disinclined to be merciful.

"Then we have no further business here." Suydam adjusted his top hat. "You will bring me more artifacts?"

The sailors looked at each other. One said, "You see what can happen?"

Suydam licked his lips. "I can't stop. I must know everything."

The sailor nodded. All three slipped down dark streets before the sun could fully rise.

Suydam studied the quivering wreck that was once Paddy McGuire, and whispered, "It may take decades, eons, but, god help me, I *will* know these secrets."

Then he, too, was gone.

RATIONALIST FEMME: PUNITIVE JUSTICE

by William E. Chambers

"**M**r. Alvarez, eleven years ago two sisters disappeared on Long Island. Hannah Brant was fourteen. Naomi was nine. You lost Naomi. I've come for Hannah."

"Si?" The raspy voice on the other end hesitated, "Who—"

"I am your judge, jury, and—unless you comply with my demands—your executioner, too."

The voice rose sharply. "I don't respond to threats, Señor."

"Delivering Hannah is your only response if you wish to live."

Kyla Quartrain was secure in her invisibility, aware her green-brown mottled camouflage scuba outfit would be visually disruptive enough to the human eye as to make the contours of her body inseparable from the upright palm trees, dense green leaves, and overall jungle foliage surrounding her.

And with scarlet rays morphing into violet streaks as dusk overpowered day, the incoming darkness provided the additional shelter needed to rock her desired objective with enough explosives to jolt Carlos Alvarez's attitude of overconfidence into a mindset of fear.

Kyla accepted risk under any combat circumstance as a deadly factor. So she felt reassured by the two 9mm semi-automatics with built-in noise suppressors fastened to her hips in watertight holsters. The Sig-Sauers's handle-fed twelve round ammo clips were accompanied by four more twelve-round magazines attached to the back of her utility belt. A retractable, hard rubber-coated grappling hook fixed to a nylon parachute cord that wound through a reel inside an intense, spring-operated, tube-shaped launcher was also clipped to the belt. Pressing unseen between her breasts beneath the diver's outfit was a gold chain and medal bearing the astrological scales of Libra—her birth sign—which she relied on to save her life once in the past. The final accoutrement was a quiver slung across her back containing a collapsible 36-inch anodized aluminum blowgun and a series of poison-tipped and tranquilizer -laden darts.

Kyla focused the laser rangefinder of her Steiner Military Binoculars on the sleek white luxury yacht idling about a quarter mile offshore. The only visible occupants were two members of the crew she spied on board, though she knew there could be more below deck. Since the orgies never started before midnight, she believed the actions she was about to commit allowed time to be her ally in this quest. Donning a diving mask and snorkel, she trotted toward shore and slithered under the tepid sea, using wide circular strokes and kicks to propel herself unobtrusively toward the vessel. Nightfall was nearly complete by the time she began her hand-over-hand ascent up the yacht's anchor chain.

Safely over the bow, Kyla extended her blowgun, inserted a tranquilizer dart then gently opened the impermeable Velcro flap of her right-hand holster and stealthily advanced toward the stern, where she had originally observed the two crew members. The scent of cigarette smoke indicated her course to be correct. Drawing closer, she heard a masculine voice talking Spanish while another laughed softly. Rounding the curve of the yacht's rail, she saw the backs of two short men in white uniforms gazing toward the open sea, half-smoked butts glowing in each of their left hands. Drawing a deep breath, she pursed her lips, raised the blowgun and exhaled forcefully toward the man farthest from her. He flinched as the dart struck the back of his neck, then swatted it as one would a mosquito. There was barely enough time to slip another tranquilizer into the weapon before her victim staggered drunkenly backwards and slumped to his knees.

The companion exclaimed something unintelligible, then rushed toward his fallen comrade but—either glimpsing or sensing a foreign presence—stopped short and pivoted rigidly toward Kyla, who immediately regretted the fear-induced tightness on the elderly man's face and released it with another burst from the blowgun. She caught the slender casualty when he started to slump, laid him gently down on the deck, and heard the man mutter 'Madre de Dios' before consciousness quit his eyes. Patting both men down, Kyla found no weapons and determined she would assure their safety once she ascertained the situation below deck. She believed poverty coerced decent people into situations they would rather avoid, and while these two worked for despicable forces they were probably victims of abominable economic circumstances. Although resolute about completing this mission, she was equally determined to uphold her moral code. If humanly possible no innocent life would be sacrificed.

Kyla reloaded the blowgun, held it ready in her left hand, then drew the 9mm from her right holster, quietly edged down the teak staircase and surveyed the dimly-lit corridor below deck. Carefully peering through each cabin door, she found them all luxuriously furnished but devoid of people. A thorough sweep of the engine room cleared her mind of worry about any more possible innocent casualties.

A glance at her Luminox diving watch indicated three hours to go before the party launches would arrive with under-aged youths of both sexes and the usually over-aged males who would pay exorbitantly for their near-pubescent services. That left plenty of time to tie the ropes she found in the engine room from the rail to the unconscious pair and lower them one at a time over the side. Once they dangled in position, she jumped overboard and maneuvered them into the motorized dinghy trailing the yacht's stern. Then she dove below and positioned the timing device to detonate the explosives she had attached to the hull the night before, and resurfaced to pilot the boat back to shore.

Kyla deposited the still-groggy men onto the beach and set the outboard engine on automatic. Then she launched the dinghy seaward and trekked back to her prearranged vantage point. Blending into the jungle's coverage, she adjusted the night-range binoculars, watched the horizon, and waited. An eternity of minutes passed before a shimmering black and orange ball billowed skyward and a roar shattered the tropical calm. Piercing overhead shrieks drew her attention to erratic shadows darting across treetops, while the undergrowth alongside her rustled frantically with unseen creatures. When oil and smoke fumes drifted inland burning her eyes and stinging her nostrils, she knew it was time to move on to phase two.

Kyla dropped her snorkel into a canvas backpack set in a wire basket on her rented bicycle's rear fender, withdrew night goggles, then mounted the English Racer and threw it into low gear for the two mile trip back to a hilltop cabin that served as one of her leased safe houses. The goggles removed any challenge to avoiding the ruts on the seldom-traveled dirt road she had carefully chosen. So she banished boredom by reflecting on her personal moral code and the human and spiritual forces that led her to adopt it.

Personally, Kyla believed Thomas Jefferson summed up God's existence succinctly when he—with the editing aid of Benjamin Franklin—noted in the preamble to the Declaration of Independence that the truth of the Creator's existence was self-evident. Rational thinking would lead you to conclude you can't have clocks without a clockmaker nor the conception of an endless universe teeming with varied forms of life without a conceiver. Considering herself a rationalist by birth—raised by parental Deists who believed the Creator's will could be determined through reason and logic—she was skeptical of any rigid ideology—religious or political—that belittled scientific scrutiny or feared judgmental inquiry. Kyla felt the motives of authoritarian figures were always questionable because in her life's experience whenever ideology overpowered reason morality seemed to work against its own ends.

And in the case of politicized government, ethics as defined by the average decent citizen is oftentimes non-existent, which caused her to reflect upon the first time she saw her older brother Dennis, in dress blue Navy Seal uniform, and how proud she was to take a photo of him.

The last time she saw Dennis he introduced her to a fellow Seal, Larry Fahey. Although both men only had five days military leave, she spent every possible moment with them. After the second day, Dennis caught the drift and managed to find time away from his best friend and his sister. She consummated her love for Larry in a Manhattan hotel room on the final night of leave and celebrated their blissful union with room service of hamburgers and champagne. Afterwards, Larry presented a gold Claddagh ring engraved with two hands holding a heart and told her, "This symbolizes our love and loyalty. When I return, I'll replace it with an even better band of gold."

"What a strange marriage proposal." Kyla felt her throat suddenly tighten as she remembered how she had laughed back then when he slipped the ring on her wedding finger. "Is this how you American Irish operate?"

Fighting back sadness, she recalled the way he rolled the tray away from the bed and said, "I'll show you how we operate…"

Kyla willed her melancholy away, Larry and Dennis were killed in the line of duty less than a month after that special night. The Quartrain family had been notified that Dennis's death was due to a training accident. An inquiry about Larry brought the same answer. Kyla assuaged her grief by determining to follow the path of these two men she so loved and admired. They were dedicated to fighting America's enemies and she silently pledged to do the same. She took to gymnastics, weight training, and yoga with the same zeal she pursued her Master's Degree in Criminology, and upon graduating John Jay College, enlisted in the Navy. She planned to serve her country through the military first, then pursue a career in law enforcement to defend society at large.

While women were not represented in the Seal units, her natural ability with weapons and the ease with which she embraced hand-to-hand combat training qualified her for Special Ops covert assignments. After demonstrating exceptional ability in several spying operations, Kyla received top secret clearance and discovered the harsh truth about Dennis and Larry's fate. They had been killed by gunfire while on a clandestine raid against a notorious drug lord in the Cayman Islands. This knowledge became especially bitter when she found that the government she now championed sacrificed her older brother and her future husband so that an equally evil narcotics kingpin could replace the one they helped take down.

This new *ally* was willing to smuggle guns to the enemies of left wing anti-American factions in various Caribbean locations. The knowledge that she lost her loved ones to such a nefarious scheme was enough to shatter the idea of fighting for genuine justice through any organized government agency. Although disillusioned by political realities, Kyla grudgingly acknowledged that sometimes one evil had to be employed against another for the greater good. Hadn't FDR reluctantly partnered with Stalin to fight Hitler? So officially accepting her discharge when it came due, she still remained in an elite Special Ops Reserve Division because it allowed her the privilege of choosing only the assignments she approved of and rejecting all others. Although retained on salary with bonuses added for each undertaking she chose—her downtime was plentiful—and the pay sufficient to allow her to fulfill the self-imposed moral obligation she righteously felt she owed to the memory of the men who she loved. Now with the freedom to pick her own private battles, she vowed to deliver punitive justice to the type of people Larry and Dennis died fighting against.

It was that sense of obligation that led her to this resort island paradise bordering Mexico and Central America, which was aptly titled Poseidon's Trident because it catered to three of the Seven Deadly Sins: Lust, Greed, and Gluttony. Lust was satiated in any and all forms through the services of youths. Less publicized entertainments were rumored available to profligate customers with sadistic or even murderous tendencies, since undocumented orphans abound in third world countries, rendering human capital cheap. Greed was catered to at gaming tables, slot machines, and betting parlors featuring bare knuckle Ultimate Fighting contests. Gluttony's role thrived through the overabundance of food, drink, and drugs.

Kyla brought the bike into her two-room cabin, braced it under the entrance knob, and shot the door's bolt. She raised the window shade and looked over the downward slope of the hill, noting a small orange glow on the otherwise dark horizon. Delving into her backpack, she snapped open her disposable cell phone and entered the military code and password which connected her to a stealth satellite signal that accommodated internet and phone communications anywhere in the world. Next she attached the acoustic coupler of a portable voice changer to the charging slot in back of the handset, adjusted the voice pitch from female to male, punched in the required digits, and waited. Within seconds a raspy male voice muttered, "Si?"

"Tonight your yacht. Tomorrow your life..." Kyla heard the hiss of his breath, "unless you deliver Hannah to me."

"Why do you want Hannah?"

Kyla's only answer was a loud impatient sigh.

"What if she doesn't wish to leave me?"

"Then you'd best make a will."

A short spell of silence was followed by, "Tell me what I must do."

Kyla's normally brown hair was now strikingly blond and her hazel eyes bright green via contact lenses. Leaving her rental car in a parking lot several blocks away, she approached the Trident Casino on foot. She wore a smart gray pants suit that accentuated her curves and pretended not to notice the leers thrown her way by the tuxedoed gaming dealers working the tables or their casually attired male customers. She approached a muscular, dark-skinned man in a white suit whose spiral corded earpiece indicated he was a member of the casino's security detail, and uttered previously agreed-to code words, "Can you tell me who I might see about a job?"

The man ushered her to an elevator that opened into Carlos Alvarez's office, where he sat behind a huge mahogany desk chomping an unlit cigar. Three tough-looking Hispanic men in seemingly mandatory white suits flanked the room strategically. Alvarez stared at Kyla a moment before gesturing toward a cushioned leather armchair. When she sat down, he said, "Who sent you?

"I don't know," she shrugged.

When half of a yellow-toothed grin appeared below his pencil thin mustache the white suits laughed scornfully. The one to the right of Alvarez spoke. "Señorita, you think my boss—he believes that? He's an imbecile?"

"I was awakened last night by a call from a man who said he would pay me three thousand dollars to come to this casino and ask for a job. I told him I was American and planning to go home and didn't want a job. He explained I would be repeating a code that would allow me to meet you and that I was to leave here with a woman. He promised me another three thousand after he collected the woman from me. It sounded phony, so I hung up on him."

Alvarez's loose jowls jigged as he shook his head. "And then, Señorita…"

"He called back and told me to look under my door where I found an envelope with thirty crisp hundred dollar bills. I can use the money—"

"If you need money you can always work for me." Alvarez's guttural laugh revealed more stained teeth and was echoed by his guards. "How do I know you're telling the truth?"

"The money's in my jacket pocket. I can—"

"Place your hands on my desk." He motioned to the man on his right. "Check her pockets." The bodyguard produced an envelope from her right hand pocket and Alvarez counted the money. He shoved the envelope across the desk to her and said, "You're in grave danger, Muchacha."

"Why?" Kyla swallowed hard and stiffened. "I'm just delivering a message—doing an errand."

"You'll do an errand, all right!" Alvarez flung the cigar into an onyx pedestal ashtray next to his desk, then stood up. "You will tell me who this man is and where we can find him!"

"I don't know…" Kyla's eyes widened. "He told me you might ask and—"

Alvarez's brandy and cigar-breath made her flinch as he leaned forward. "Do you think I'll just hand over one of my employees after my life has been threatened and my yacht bombed! I have you now. He'll see me on my terms or you'll live in a hell that Dante himself could not even imagine!"

"Señor Alvarez…Please… He told me that you might not cooperate and said I should—"

"Cooperate!" Alvarez's egg-shaped body undulated as he shouted, "You should know what—"

"Explain that he would listen to our conversation and respond accordingly."

"Listen?"

Kyla's lifted her pant leg and revealed the power pack strapped to her calf. "I'm wearing a wire. He left it outside my door with written instructions on how to use it."

Alvarez swayed side to side, then slumped like a deflating balloon into his swivel chair and dropped his face into his hands. Silence enveloped the office only to be broken by the tremors in his voice when he finally lifted his head revealing suddenly mottled jowls and half whispered, "Domingo…"

The bodyguard on his right said, "Yes, Boss?"

"What do you think we should do?"

A trace of frown crossed Domingo's rugged features as he answered, "Hannah's expendable."

Hannah Brant's arm felt rigid as Kyla gripped it and escorted her hastily toward the car. The lovely young woman, clad in a colorful shift and high heels, obeyed silently when ordered to accompany this stranger, yet her blue eyes seemed glazed and her smile strangely serene. When they reached the parking lot, she asked, "Que pasa, Señorita?"

"Please get in the car. And do speak English."

"Carlos told me I must obey you." Once seated, Kyla turned toward the woman and did a quick body search. Hannah's glaze remained placid. "Am I to entertain you?"

"No."

Silence prevailed for the rest of the journey. Once inside her cabin, Kyla said, "Hannah, I apologize for what I did in the car. I want to be your friend."

"Who are you?"

"I've come to take you away from here."

"This island?"

"This whole life—if you wish to go."

A light seemed to flicker in her otherwise empty eyes. "Did you buy me?"

"No. No one will ever buy you or take you by force again. If you do what I say you'll go home to America. You'll be free. Do you wish it?"

The light receded from Hannah's eyes. "Why are they—and you—testing me, Señorita?"

"No one is testing you, Hannah." Kyla gently caressed the girl's face. "I know what they did to you and I can take you to freedom and safety—if you wish it."

"Of course I wish it." Hannah's hands crossed her chest, polished fingernails glinting like rubies in the muted glow of a kerosene lamp. "But we will never leave this place alive."

"I can handle these people." Kyla knew she had to bolster Hannah's confidence fast if her plan was to work, so she added, "Hannah, I blew up Carlos's yacht and I can save you, too."

"It was you?" An invisible hand seemed to twist Hannah's serene features. "You—a woman—did all that?"

"Yes," Kyla nodded. "Now will you trust me?"

"I've learned I can't trust men..." A rapid blink replaced Hannah's usual stare. "But if you can do all that—I must trust you!"

"Excellent. All our needs are in these two canvas backpacks."

Staring curiously as Kyla opened one pack, shucked her pants outfit and climbed into the garb she wore on Alvarez's vessel, Hannah muttered, "Buen Jesús ..."

"Good Jesus has nothing to do with this. As you see, I'm qualified to protect you." Kyla slipped night goggles around her neck and threw a blouse, jeans, and boots to Hannah. "Lose the clothes and put these on. I have a deep sea fisherman on retainer waiting in a secluded cove a couple of miles from here. Your captors are scared and uncertain right now and I'm counting on that confusion to get us back to the Mexican mainland."

As Hannah changed, Kyla noted the Egyptian pyramid, a symbol of universal power with its all-seeing eye, tattooed to her left breast.

"Señori—uh—ma'am, I don't even know your name."

"Call me Kay."

"I'm ready, Kay."

"Follow me." Kyla swung one canvas backpack over each shoulder. "We're leaving through the back window."

Hannah's chest heaved and perspiration glowed like tiny diamonds on her face by the time Kyla motioned her to stop near the crest of a thirty-to-forty foot high ridge. Moonlight splayed pale yellow beams over calmly rolling ocean waves below as Kyla dropped the canvas backpacks and punched a code into her cell phone. When the text was returned she said, "He's ready for us."

"But..." Hannah's curious stare returned. "There's no vessel in sight."

"It's tucked in an alcove under this ridge. You rested enough to go?"

"Si—I mean yes..."

"Then let's go. Want to be back by daybreak."

One of the first skills Kyla learned as a covert operator was how to identify and network with government agencies and independent collaborators domestically and on foreign soil. So she had bribe money ready in case of intervention by Mexican authorities or seafaring drug dealers, but the short cruise back to the mainland went unchallenged. Dressed back in civilian clothes, she paid the vessel's captain and hailed a cab from the boat dock to the condo she had rented in Acapulco under the name Kay Pearsall.

Trained to know that successful infiltration requires advance knowledge of terrain, and a variety of safe houses if available, Kyla observed every precaution to better her chances of success. Once safely inside the condo, she ordered breakfast delivered from a nearby restaurant and watched the news while they ate. The sinking of the yacht "El Amor Siempre" or "Love Always" was the main subject of debate by local media, with theories ranging from rogue gangs demanding protection money to rival flesh-trade competitors muscling in on Señor Alvarez's action. Kyla noted that one talking head came closest to the truth by spinning the idea that someone might want to draw attention to the fact that while adult prostitution is legal in Mexico, the debasement of children is not. That show ended with an interview whereby Señor Alvarez claimed all his employees were legal age and that he thought the United States was trying to deflect its immigration problems by fomenting public opinion hostile to its southern border neighbors.

Kyla motioned Hannah to get comfortable on the living room settee while she sat facing her in a cane-backed chair, then said, "You know the Internet makes any agenda hard to hide any more. Anyone can find out about child prostitution or anything else with the strike of a key these days. That's how I became emotionally concerned about you and your sister. While surfing, I found a story released on an anonymous blog about a missionary nun who ran a hospice in one of the barrios and treated a young American girl suffering with AIDS. She said the girl's name was Naomi Brant and that Naomi explained how she and her sister were deceived as children into leaving their home in Long Island and forced into prostitution in Mexico. The nun reported Naomi's claim to the local police and the town newspaper. The story was never officially printed, although a version was circulated by an underground press, and a few days after that the nun almost died at the hands of a hit-and-run driver while walking to the marketplace."

Hannah stared woodenly, then asked, "Is my sister still alive, Kay?"

"Don't know…" Kyla frowned. "A nurse found her bed empty the morning after the nun's *accident.*"

"I see."

"Do you know where she was working before she tried to escape?"

"No." Hannah curled into a semi-fetal position and lowered her head. Her long red hair framed her face as she murmured, "Only that Carlos sent her away."

Kyla continued, "My next internet research proved indeed that you and Naomi had disappeared from Long Island. Many news articles covered the story at the time. I even contacted your mother."

"My mother! How—is she?"

"Not well. Cancer. Receiving chemo treatments."

"Still smoking?"

"Yes."

"And my father?"

Kyla hesitated. "Uh…"

"Drunk?"

"Afraid so."

"Maybe I can help them—if I get back home."

"When. Not if," Kyla assured her. "Now on to the big picture."

"Que—what?"

Kyla walked into the bedroom and returned with a digital camcorder and tripod. While setting the equipment up she said, "I'm going to tape an interview with you about your abduction and the child abuse in Poseidon's Trident. Some internet blogs claim even torture and murder urges can be gratified for a price. Tell me everything you know, then I'll email it to major media outlets. When they respond we'll arrange for a public news conference right here in Acapulco. After telling your story you'll demand asylum in our embassy until you can be escorted home safely by American authorities. The publicity should generate enough outrage to shame the Mexican government and hopefully prod the United States and the U.N. to take action against these thugs."

Hannah revealed a host of sordid details into the camcorder and Kyla shot it right through the internet. Fifteen minutes later, the first phone call came to her throwaway cell phone. She handed it to Hannah who set the time and place for a public interview. Several more news outlets contacted her within the hour and she gave them all the same appointment. Then she showered, put on fresh clothes, and said, "I'm ready to go, Kay."

"Good luck."

"Aren't you coming?"

"No. My work's done. I'll disappear now. It's your show. Again, good luck."

Kyla stepped onto the balcony and squinted against the morning sun to watch Hannah walk down the oceanfront street toward the hotel where she was to hold her outdoor press conference. A small crowd of reporters were loitering in front with several satellite vans in anticipation of the upcoming event. Hannah stopped momentarily and drew a cell phone from the pocket of her jeans. Kyla realized she had forgotten to take that phone back. An unsettled feeling kicked in when she saw Hannah dial a number and become engaged in conversation. Minutes later, Hannah pocketed the phone and continued on to the hotel.

Kyla sensed trouble and loaded up her backpacks while watching the live TV interview. Hannah's features registered no emotion as she looked into the camera and said, "Before I take any questions I have to tell everyone that the message I put on the internet was false. I was being held against my will by a woman named Kay who threatened to kill me if I didn't make that video. My sister and I were never coerced into anything. We ran away from home because it was miserable there. We made our way to Mexico and worked as dishwashers and waitresses until we were old enough to become prostitutes—which, by the way is legal in Mexico and pays very well. I believe my captor is an American operative whose agenda is to discredit the present Mexican authorities for political reasons that I can't understand."

Kyla snapped the TV off as reporters began hurling questions. She counted on intuition to tell her which way to play this surprising and unfortunate turn. She tucked one pistol under the waistband of her jeans and covered it with a loose fitting blouse. If pursued by Alvarez's thugs, killing would not be a problem. But fighting with police was out since they were just doing their jobs. She hefted the canvas backpacks, one containing her weapons, the other various portable necessities such as the snorkel, camcorder, laptop, and other electronic items, then headed through the door to the stairwell, which would make for a faster exit than the elevator. But the sounds of tramping boots and the squawk of two-way radios sent her back into the room and out to the balcony. Her condo door shook under a heavy knock and a stern voice shouted, "Policía! Abre la puerta!"

Kyla whipped open the grappling hook from the weapons backpack, thrust it into the portable launcher and aimed for the roof. The grapple careened upward past two balconies and hooked the groove of a terracotta tile. She then slung that backpack on, abandoned the other one and jumped off the balcony. Planting both feet on the stucco wall, she climbed upward to the sound of wood splintering inside the condo and someone shouting, "Policia! Open! Surrender—"

Kyla reached the peak of the slanted rooftop before she heard yelling on her balcony below. That same commanding voice issued orders to look for her in the stairwell and watch the elevators in the lobby. She managed to quietly scramble over the many adjoining rooftops she had mapped out in advance to another building, where a brunette named Laura Jeffries rented an apartment. Opening the roof hatch gingerly, she peered into the empty stairwell below and quickly descended three flights until she reached her floor. A thirty-something couple with two young boys nodded as she passed their elevator bank. She killed time by a vending machine until they boarded, then entered her apartment. Now was the time to shower, limber up with yoga stretches and meditate. Tomorrow a woman with a black pixie hairstyle and dark brown eyes would emerge into the Acapulco sunshine to seek another path to success in a mission that today had gone awry.

Sor Maria?"

The ancient crevices of a weathered face writhed like awakened snakes as a wheelchair-bound woman glanced up at Kyla. "Norteamericano?"

"Si."

"I teach—taught English." Tight lips smiled toothlessly. "Yes. I am Sister Maria."

"My name is Laura Jeffries. May I sit?"

The nun favored the single bed beside her with a wave of a blue-veined hand over the rickety chair her visitor was about to use. "Sit there, please."

"I am a freelance journalist," Kyla explained, "and I know about your involvement with Naomi Brant."

"That is why I am crippled in this chair." Curling both arms under her threadbare poncho the nun shivered, although no breeze crossed the stuffy little bedroom. "Satan has Méjico by the throat. I am also—was a nurse. I tried to save that child…"

"I know. I read about it."

"Si—yes. I reported her story to authorities." The nun's watery eyes fixated on Kyla's face. "Were you the one who tried to rescue Hannah recently?"

Kyla never flinched from Sister Maria's stare. "No."

"Our sisters go to the marketplace. News travels." The nun's eyes shifted to the crucifix on the wall above the side of her bed, then back to Kyla. "Domingo Melendez rules the very souls of those poor girls."

"Domingo! I thought Alvarez—"

"Clever Domingo leads everyone to believe that." The nun slowly shook her head. "Alvarez is a scapegoat. The one *you* want is Domingo."

Kyla's eyebrows twitched at the nun's implication, but her voice remained unperturbed. "Did Naomi tell authorities about Domingo's *true* criminal status?"

"Yes. But Domingo had himself edited out of all reports. Even the underground got the information wrong."

"Please tell me everything you can about Domingo—especially his personal habits if you know of any—to help me expose him to the world."

The drive back from the barrio to the luxurious dwellings of Acapulco Bay took about two hours. Kyla mulled over the details of mind persuasion Sister Maria had related as employed by Domingo. Blondes, redheads, and other light-skinned women were especially rare in bordellos south of the American border and fetched top-dollar fees. But they had to be kept under control by means other than physically destructive drugs, and Domingo discovered the way to do that.

Food and sleep deprivation, chanting, lengthened contemplation, and hours of one-on-one interrogation followed by group gatherings persuaded newly-abducted members that a better life lay before them if they would renounce themselves to a greater cause. This explained Hannah's betrayal. She had been unhappy at home, had dysfunctional parents and fell under Domingo's persuasion somehow in Long Island. In turn, Hannah excited Naomi with promises of a better life if she accompanied her and Domingo to Mexico. Naomi went willingly and succumbed to the spell of Domingo's mind-control programs. But when she contracted AIDS from a high-paying customer who refused to use sexual protection, she was relegated to the lowest brothels of the island. Disgusted by this life, she somehow found a way to escape and ended up at the Catholic shelter.

Kyla reflected on how Thomas Jefferson once said: *The tree of liberty must be refreshed from time to time with the blood of patriots and tyrants.*

Dennis and Larry had been patriots and Domingo Melendez was a tyrant. Benjamin Franklin also noted 'that rebellion to tyrants is obedience to God.' These ageless sayings bolstered her determination to strike whatever blow she could against evil, without suffering the pangs of guilt associated with unbridled revenge. While Domingo's death might not destroy his empire or free its present captives, the loss of his charismatic talents would certainly impede its expansion and perhaps prevent the enslavement of more young people in the future. Now the task ahead was to combine logic with intuition and draft a workable plan.

Kyla returned to her apartment carrying a list of Domingo's habits in her bag. The nun had learned a lot from Naomi, and Kyla felt she could blend in at the clubs and restaurants he frequented until an opportunity to take him down presented itself. Stepping into the room, she intuitively felt, rather than saw, a figure behind the door. Swiveling about she launched a kick that fell short when a jolt of power knocked her to the floor. She heard herself moan as flames seemed to engulf her every pore and corpuscle. Hands gripped her arms, dragged her, then threw her down. She blinked through eyes that seemed clogged with sand until the vision of a grinning man appeared hovering over her and a familiar voice said, "Saludos,

Puta! Do you not know I have eyes everywhere? Why would a well-off American visit a missionary nun in a barrio unless it was to make trouble? Informers know I pay well. I received a call with your rental's license plate number and traced you to this place, Laura Jeffries—or whoever the hell you are!"

"That's Kay." A feminine voice chimed in. "She looks different, but I recognized the sound of her voice when she moaned. And the nose and lips…that's Kay."

"I went through your canvas backpack, Kay, and found your nice toys. I like toys myself. Especially my Taser, which I am going to use to extract the truth about who employs you after we return to my quarters at Poseidon. But first I have to help restore your bodily functions so you can bring me pleasure. Hannah, help me take her clothes off, then—"

"Por qué Domingo? She is not one of us…"

"Do not question me!"

"Lo sentimos, Domingo."

"Sorry isn't good enough. Do as you're told!"

"Si."

"And speak English. I want this bitch to understand us."

Kyla's muscles convulsed as the clothing was stripped from her body. Then Domingo held her head while Hannah spoon-fed an orange liquid into her mouth. After a while, the liquid began to relax her muscles and restore a feeling of physical normalcy. When she was able to sit up on the bed, Domingo said, "Emergen-C is one great product with its powerful combination of electrolytes and vitamins. Now you'll be normal enough to appreciate my passion."

Domingo chose one of Kyla's pistols from her canvas backpack, removed the safety, and slid a round into the firing chamber. Then he handed it to Hannah, saying, "This Sig-Sauer is silenced. All you have to do is point and squeeze the trigger. If she resists me in any way do just that."

Grinning down at Kyla he began to unzip his white linen trousers, when Hannah said, "Domingo! She is—ella es sucio—unclean!"

"I told you not to question my actions!"

"But we…those chosen…are only worthy of you. She is not!"

Domingo's grin faded as his head swiveled toward Hannah. "Question me once more and you'll end up working the barrio's streets like your sister…"

Kyla wanted to turn Hannah's disquiet to her own advantage by attacking Domingo while he was distracted and chance convincing Hannah to rethink her loyalty to him. But she couldn't summon enough strength to be effective. The helplessness that engulfed her as he turned back was somewhat ameliorated when she realized he hadn't removed the Libra charm from around her neck. So she made the sign of the cross as he leaned over to fondle her breasts. That religious ritual brought a chuckle from him as he brushed her lips with his, then said, "Do you think Jesus is going to save you?"

Kyla's answer was to bring her fingers from her forehead to her chest again instead of continuing the sacred gesture but she gripped the Libra charm and jerked it toward his face. She pressed the back of the medal while holding her own breath. Vapor hissed from the bottom of the charm and Domingo's eyes widened in panic. He spun from her and stood gasping, then made gurgling sounds and tottered away from the bed to fall face down on the floor. Kyla's eyes locked with Hannah's. The young woman was still pointing the gun in her direction, but now tears marred her usual glaze, and anguish distorted her normally serene features. Kyla spoke softly, "Hannah, please…Give me the gun—"

"No!" Kyla flinched at Hannah's half scream. "Is Domingo dead?"

"No, Hannah—"

"Is he dead?"

"He's alive…unconscious…if you look…he's breathing…"

Hannah's aim never wavered from Kyla as she knelt by Domingo and started to sob. Rising she said, "He is alive…"

"I told y—"

"He swore nev—" Sobs convulsed her voice. "Never to touch any woman who wasn't an initiate."

"He lied to you, Hannah." Kyla watched the gun tremble in the weeping woman's two-handed grip and wondered if she could muster the strength to dive for the weapon, then decided verbal persuasion was a far safer gamble. "Hannah, please. Give me the gun."

"No!"

Kyla froze as Hannah cocked the weapon, then swung it toward Domingo's prostrate frame. The pistol coughed softly and Domingo's body jerked. Blood welled up from a puncture in his back. Then the weapon spoke once more and blood burst from his head. A low wail escaped Hannah's throat as the semi-automatic slid from her lowered hands and plunked against the floorboards. "Naomi...Oh God...what have I caused..."

Kyla stared through the high window of her brownstone and watched the first snow of winter dust the quiet Greenpoint Brooklyn side street. Then, raising a tumbler of Jameson's to the photos on the mantle over her fireplace, she saluted the figures of the uniformed men who she so loved and sipped the iced drink. Larry introduced her to the Irish whiskey and she hoped he was returning the toast from the other side of the vale. She placed the glass between the pictures, stared at the gold Claddagh ring on her finger and reflected over the accomplishments of her mission. Domingo's betrayal of his own false ideology shattered Hannah's blind faith and saved Kyla's life. Bringing the guilt-ridden woman back to America on the same chartered fishing boat that originally brought Kyla and her weaponry into Mexico turned out to be uneventful.

During various covert operations, Kyla made acquaintances both home and abroad with mind-control experts. So after convincing Hannah to agree to enroll in an emotional trauma curriculum, she gave her two thousand dollars for personal necessities, then placed the woman in the custody of a freelance cult deprogrammer who was often employed by the CIA and paid him in advance for his services. Hannah understood "Kay" was fading from her existence and tearfully expressed appreciation for her rescue and new chance in life.

Kyla mulled accepting a government assignment soon because her funds were drawing low. She felt her goals were worth the expense and trusted her American heroes Jefferson and Franklin would agree. She believed both these brilliant personages would applaud her methods and approve of her accomplishments. While Larry and Dennis would have probably been displeased about her leading their type of lifestyle, she was sure they would also have been positively impressed by her achievements. And if Franklin was correct in his assessment of rebellion to tyrants, then God should be pleased as well.

THE WOMAN

by Mackenzie Clarkes

To Mister Holmes,
The maiden Irene
Was London's
Dame of crime
Her sapphire eyes
Did outshine
The fair ladies
Of London's fame.

REFLECTION OF GUILT

by Laird Long

Ray Miller rushed up to the sheriff's deputies as soon as they pulled into his empty driveway. The tall, lean pensioner jerked the rear door of the patrol car open and folded his long frame inside. "They just stole it!" he yelled. "Let's—"

"Your car, Mr. Miller?" Deputy Sheriff Tina Jessup asked, turning around in the front seat to look at the flustered man.

"Right! The Ray Miller! My 1968 Dodge Polara."

Deputy Sheriff Brendan Thomas grinned behind the wheel. "That cherry-red vintage car with 'Ray Miller' stenciled in big white letters on both sides?"

Everybody in town knew about Miller's car, how much he loved it, and the fact he'd named it after himself.

"That's right!" the man shouted. "Hurry up! Let's go!"

"Go where?" Jessup asked. "Did you see who took your vehicle? Where they went?"

"No," Miller admitted. "But I saw those two punks, Pete Tillis and Jerry Spruce, hanging around down the street, eyeing the Ray Miller while I was polishing him. And then when I went into the backyard for a couple of minutes and came back, the car and the punks were gone!"

"You think they took it?" Thomas said, looking at Miller in the rearview mirror.

"Yeah, Mutt and Jeff! Who else?"

Both deputies chuckled. The difference in height between the two young men *was* striking and humorous. Pete Tillis towered over the diminutive Jerry Spruce.

Deputy Thomas shifted the patrol car into reverse and backed out of the driveway. "Well, they shouldn't be hard to find—driving *that* car in *this* town."

"Exactly!" Miller agreed. "So step on it!"

They drove down the main drag, out onto the county highway. And sure enough, about half a mile up the road, the bright red paint job of Ray Miller's vintage car was clearly visible in the afternoon sunshine. What wasn't visible from that distance was who was driving the stolen vehicle.

Thomas tromped on the accelerator and Jessup switched on the lights and siren, giving chase.

The stolen car rounded a bend up ahead, hidden from view by the woods on either side of the highway. When the patrol car whipped around the same corner, the trio inside found the Ray Miller parked by the side of the road, empty.

"They can't have gone far!" Deputy Jessup yelped, leaping out of the police vehicle. Her partner and the angry car owner followed at her heels.

Five minutes later, the two police officers and Ray Miller emerged from the woods, along with Pete Tillis and Jerry Spruce. The two young men were in handcuffs.

"Okay, who was driving?" Deputy Thomas asked the pair, when they'd all arrived back at the parked cars.

Pete Tillis looked over, and down, at Jerry Spruce. Jerry looked up at Pete. Neither one responded to the deputy's question. They both knew the driver of the stolen vehicle would be facing the more serious charges.

"Punks!" Ray Miller growled. Then the elderly man hustled over to his car, pulled the passenger-side door open and slid inside on the front benchseat, happy to get his car back, but worried about any damage.

"Mr. Miller! Wait!" Deputy Jessup yelled.

Too late. Miller had slipped in under the large steering wheel, was running his hands caressingly over the wheel and the dashboard of his namesake, erasing any fingerprints. He completed the job by reaching out and adjusting the rearview mirror upwards until it suited him, then getting out of the car on the driver's side and using the door handle to close that door.

"Well, there goes any chance of dusting for prints," Deputy Thomas stated. "Unless one of these two confesses, or we can find a witness, we'll never know who was driving the car."

Deputy Jessup smiled, watching Ray Miller lovingly polish the hood of his car with a chamois. "I know who was at the wheel of the Ray Miller."

"Who!?" Thomas and Miller both asked.

"Jerry Spruce," Jessup answered, looking at the small man. "I observed tall Mr. Miller adjust the rearview mirror of his recovered vehicle upwards to see out of it properly, when he got into his car. Indicating that the most recent driver had adjusted the mirror downward to fit his shorter height. Pete Tillis isn't short."

Jerry Spruce hung his head, the joyride most definitely over.

✗

THE ADVENTURE OF THE NINE HOLE LEAGUE

by John J. White

Baker Street, London
18 June, 1892

I cannot explain the severity of my shock when, for the first time since my acquaintance with my good friend Mr Sherlock Holmes, I observed him weeping.

It had been several days since Holmes solved the difficult, but not impossibly difficult, case of The Nine Hole League, which I will describe in detail from my diary, where I chronicle all of the adventures on which I accompany Holmes.

I rang the bell several times at 221B Baker Street, the address of the renowned sleuth and formerly my own residence as well, before my plunge into the happy arms of matrimony with the beloved Mrs Watson, *née* Morstan.

Knowing Mrs Hudson was visiting her nephew in Salisbury, leaving Holmes to his rather slovenly bachelor habits, I waited patiently for my companion to throw open his window and ejaculate, *Come in, Doctor! Come in!* But I am sorry to say that did not happen.

Instead, fearing my friend might have come to some harm owing to the influence of his rather disturbing habits, I let myself in and quickly ascended the seventeen steps to Holmes's apartment. After a hard knocking on his study door, with no reply, I let my imaginings consume me and burst into the locked room, slightly harming my shoulder in the process.

Holmes sat slumped in an armchair by the unlit fireplace, his deerstalker hat pulled back and askew on his head, the unmistakably pungent odour of opium filling the dark room.

Tears streamed down his face as my usually stoic mentor sobbed uncontrollably. That damned opium. I thought he had rid himself of it, but I had misjudged. I grabbed his shoulders and tried to shake him to his senses.

"Holmes," said I. "My dear sir, come out of it! What is the matter? What is the cause of this? Come out of it, I beg you!"

Holmes looked up at me through the smoky haze.

"Watson. Oh, that you should see me in such condition, my dear friend."

I removed his cap and went to the cabinet to fetch some brandy. After he sipped it, he sat back in the chair and wiped his eyes.

"What is it, Holmes? I am your friend, you know that, sir. Discretion will be utmost, of course. What puts you in this state?"

Holmes sipped more brandy and then sighed.

"It is because of her, my friend."

✗   ✗   ✗   ✗

Baker Street, London
Seven days earlier
11 June, 1892

I was summoned by messenger to my old bachelor residence, a matter of some urgency, according to the note from Holmes. After greeting Mrs Hudson at the door, she and I stepped lively up to Holmes's study, where Holmes waved his hand for patience whilst continuing to puzzle over one of the chemical experiments that always demanded his keen attention.

"Well, sir," said I. "The urgency of the matter seems to have abated, if I were to surmise."

"Yes, yes, Watson. I am quite finished now and sincerely apologise for taking you from your patient. A rather large wound, I assume, from the strong odour of carbolic acid emanating from your jacket."

I sat in an armchair across from my friend, who now did likewise.

"Your powers of observation are as sharp as ever. Now. The pressing matter?"

"Not quite so pressing, Watson, but instead, a need of your services and knowledge. You are still a golfer of note at London Scottish, I assume."

I laughed. "Well, I wouldn't say *of note*, Holmes, but when my duties to my practice and Mrs Watson are not so dear, I will slip away for a round now and then. You should join me sometime.

Give you something to do with your time besides this morbid fascination with the criminal society. Yes, you must."

"I know little of the game, which is exactly why I called for you. You have read, no doubt, of the unfortunate murder of Lord Douglas Fletcher."

I had, indeed, read of it, and it was some point of interest in the clubhouse at London Scottish. "Killed with his own golf club, by his caddie," said I. "A hard man, they say, this Fletcher. No one's friend at my club. Said to cheat and bully, but hardly a reason to end a man's life. There was talk his title was somewhat suspect, I hear."

Holmes relit his pipe and blew smoke to the gilded ceiling before responding.

"Precisely, Watson. It seems in Scotland, now, anyone owning the slightest quantity of land finds himself honoured with the title of lord. The Yard is investigating the man's past. But now—why *we* are involved."

"Yes. I was wondering when you would get to the matter at hand. What have we to do with the Lord Fletcher murder?"

Holmes pointed to the stairwell. "There is a young lady, a Miss O'Reilly, from whom I have received a rather lengthy letter pleading for her fiancé, the infamous caddie charged with crushing the side of Lord Fletcher's head with a—spoon, I believe you call it?"

"Yes, that is what it is called," said I.

"Well, Miss O'Reilly proclaims her beau's innocence and, in her desperation, has begged my services—and I, in turn, yours. And from the sound of the footsteps ascending, I believe that is her now."

Holmes stood to greet Mrs Hudson and a ravishingly beautiful girl whose yellowish brown hair peeked from a large hat common to the working class. Were I to guess, I would put her in the employ of a family, perhaps as a governess, as the hem of her plain dress was somewhat tattered. I feared should Holmes accept this commission, he would likely not receive even his expenses from this poor thing.

Before Holmes could introduce either himself or me, the young miss threw her arms around Holmes and kissed him soundly on his cheek. Amidst Holmes's scarlet blush, she continued to embrace him while she exclaimed in a strong Irish brogue, "Oh, Mr

Holmes. When I received your telegram asking me to come, I knew absolutely that you would prove Charlie's innocence. I am certain, knowing your reputation and good graces. Thank God for you, sir." She backed away from Holmes, much to his obvious relief, and turned to me.

"I'm sorry, sir," said she, her bright blue eyes dancing as she spoke. Whoever this Charlie was, I thought him a very lucky fellow.

Holmes gestured to me. "This, Miss O'Reilly, is Dr John Watson, my associate. You can feel quite comfortable speaking in his presence as he is quite discreet in all cases on which we collaborate."

She jumped to embrace me as she had Holmes, placing a loud kiss on my cheek. I may have held her a bit longer than is proper, but the young miss had a very narrow waist as well as a full bosom which, I must say, felt quite comforting to a man of my age.

"Dr Watson!" she exclaimed. "I have read of you many times and it is so kind of you to help me in my time of need."

She again pressed to embrace me, but I backed away for fear of losing my composure and embarrassing myself, perhaps even returning her kiss. Holmes came to my rescue this time; I am sure he saw my dilemma.

"Please, Miss O'Reilly, sit in this armchair. Tea?"

"Yes, please," said she, straightening her pleats. Holmes raised his eyebrows to Mrs Hudson.

"Yes, sir. I'll fetch a pot," said Mrs Hudson, shaking her head at our guest and raising her brows to Holmes in return.

We talked pleasantries of weather and her journey from Eltham to Baker Street until Mrs Hudson had returned with the tea. No sooner had Mrs Hudson left when Miss O'Reilly broke down and leaned over to cry in Holmes's lap.

Holmes looked like a young lad at his first dance and tried unsuccessfully to raise her from her embarrassing pose. I once again intervened, tapping the young lady on the shoulder. She finally sat back in her chair. I could not help but enjoy my friend's discomfort.

"Now, now, Miss O'Reilly," said Holmes. "Please sip some tea to calm yourself and tell your story to us, for the benefit of the good doctor to whom I have not yet read your letter." Holmes patted the young girl's rough hands. "There, there. Whenever you are ready."

Miss O'Reilly placed her teacup in the saucer.

"Thank you, sir. As I wrote, me Charlie and—excuse me—my fiancé, Charles Daley, and I ate a bit of lunch in the clubhouse kitchen just before he were to caddy for the Lord Fletcher, himself, though Charlie had asked not to because of his brother, Frankie, and all."

"Quite so," said Holmes. "I believe you wrote Lord Fletcher had a great deal to do with the dismissal of your fiancé's brother earlier in the week."

"Yes, sir, he did, indeed, and that's why Charlie didn't want to caddy for the man, but the master said there were no one else around at the time and ordered him to do it, no matter. He agreed but was angry, as you can well imagine. Lord Fletcher accused little Frankie-boy of calling him a cheater and demanded the club release him immediately, you see. They did, of course, Lord Fletcher being a lord and a man of wealth and all."

"And *did* your fiancé's brother call him a cheat?" I asked.

"No, sir! Frankie caught him cheating in a match against Mr Albert Tenant, another member, sir. Lord Fletcher took an illegal drop and wanted Frankie to say that it was legal and Frankie-boy would not, God bless him. You see, sir, there was a good deal of money bet—excuse me sir—wagered on the game."

Holmes looked quizzically at me. "Illegal drop?" he asked.

"You are penalised one stroke, and sometimes two strokes, when your ball is out of bounds," said I. "One drops the ball and assesses the penalty to the score. It sounds as if Lord Fletcher removed his ball from a hazard of some type and dropped it on a flat lie where he could easily hit a good shot."

"A cheat," said Holmes.

"Yes, sir!" exclaimed Miss O'Reilly. "A cheat he was, sir, and if any man deserved what he got, it was him, God rest his soul, but my Charlie would never had done somethin' such as that. He might have said he wished him dead and all, but he told me in the kitchen he wanted only to talk to his Lordship, to ask him to let Frankie back in, for God knows the family can use the money. Charlie hated Lord Fletcher, but he would not kill him. Charlie would not step on a bug, God bless him."

"And has Mr Daley spoken to you since?" asked Holmes.

"Why, sir, my Charlie told me the whole story from his cell. He planned to ask Lord Fletcher near the eighteenth."

"Eighteenth?" asked Holmes.

"The last hole in a series of holes," I explained.

"I see," said Holmes. "Please continue, Miss."

"Well, they never got there, sir. You see the Lord Fletcher always hits the ball off to the right on number eleven hole, a four par, and there's a good lot of trees there near the Blackheath Clubhouse."

"Near the clubhouse, you say," said Holmes.

"Yes, sir. Very near. And like always, the Lord Fletcher searches for his ball so that he's not penalised and he, of course, finds it every time and pops it out on the short grass. Everyone knows he throws a new ball out as my Charlie will swear, knowing the man falsely uses another ball he keeps in his pocket. So this time, Charlie tells me, Lord Fletcher calls out to him that, of course, he has found the ball and so Charlie waits, like always, for it to miraculously come flyin' out of the woods, but instead he hears three or four sharp cracks and a yell of a sort. Charlie, he waits a while and then calls out for Lord Fletcher but hears no reply, he does. So Charlie goes into the woods, and what's there but the man dead or unconscious, he did not know, but the side of his head all covered with blood, you know."

"Did your fiancé say which side?" asked Holmes.

"Which side of what, sir?"

"Of his head. On which side of the head was the wound?"

"Oh, that. Yes, sir. This side." She touched the left side of her head. "And then Charlie, scared like he was, left the clubs and bag there and ran to the caddie master for help, he did."

"The lad should have gone to the clubhouse, where perhaps a doctor was available," said I.

"No, sir, Dr Watson. I mean, yes, sir, but my Charlie was afraid they would blame him if he went there, because of Frankie-boy and all, and they would and did, you know, but he is innocent, I know he is. Oh, Mr Holmes."

Again, she left her chair and lay her head in Holmes's lap. I gently lifted her back.

"He did not do it, sir," said she through tears. "You do not believe he did, do you, sir?"

Holmes said nothing for a moment and did not speak until he had taken three puffs of contemplation on the clay pipe.

"No, Miss O'Reilly, I do not believe Mr Daley committed the crime."

"Why is that, Holmes?" I asked.

"Well, Watson, how could someone who is about to marry one as lovely as our Miss O'Reilly risk incarceration by committing a murder with nothing to gain from the act. And besides, he went for help when he surely could have run away. Now, Miss O'Reilly, may I ask, is Mr Daley right or left-handed?"

"Right, sir."

"Yes, as I thought he might be. Thank you for coming on such short notice. You can be assured Dr Watson and I will be on the train in the morning, headed for Eltham, where I am quite certain we will soon prove Mr Daley's innocence to the local constabularies."

Miss O'Reilly bounded into Holmes's arms and, once again, kissed him with such affection, I believe Holmes was set to run from the room.

"Thank you, sir. Oh, thank you, thank you!" The pretty thing prattled on until Mrs Hudson politely closed the outside door.

Holmes turned to me. "Now, Watson. Explain this foolish game to me and spare no details."

And so, for the next few hours, that is what I did.

The next day I met Holmes at his residence and we shared a ride to the train station. Though the coal smoke blocked much of the view, it was a pleasant trip to Eltham. We rented a hansom to Royal Blackheath, where we met as prearranged with the tall, fair-haired, always eager, and always skeptical, Inspector Gregson of Scotland Yard.

"Good morning, Holmes, Dr Watson," said he. "I am afraid this is a waste of yours and the Yard's time. The boy has not confessed as yet, but it is, if I may use a cliché, an open and shut case. The young Mr Daley was overheard in the clubhouse kitchen commenting that Lord Fletcher deserved to die for his cheating and bullying, and his part in the termination of one Francis Daley from the services of the club. That, and the blood on the lad's hands and inside his fingernails made our work quite the easier, Holmes."

"Ah, Inspector," said Holmes. "As usual you have come to a conclusion that fits your hypothesis. When will the obvious points of the case steer you not to the obvious, but to the truth?"

"Yes, yes," said Gregson, merely abiding Holmes's criticism. "Now, how may I be of assistance to the *famous* Sherlock Holmes and his faithful assistant, Dr Watson?"

Holmes strode towards the clubhouse. "First sir, I would like to observe the scene of the crime. I believe Miss O'Reilly said it was the eleventh grassway?"

"Fairway, Holmes," said I.

"Yes—fairway. I believe it is close, yes?"

"Right this way, Holmes," said Gregson. "Mind yourself. You will not want one of the fine members of the Royal to punt a gutta-percha aside your brilliant head, now."

"Gutta-percha?" asked Holmes.

"A golf ball, Holmes," said I.

"Ah, yes. Fascinating sport. Like cricket, only boring."

We walked three hundred feet or so to the wooded area lining the eleventh fairway where so many of the members struck their wayward shots. Pushing aside large bushes, we found where Lord Fletcher met his unenviable end.

"This is it, all right," said the inspector. "The body was found here, still warm, by the caddie master. Mr Daley brought him right to it, being the murderer and what."

"Alleged," said Holmes.

"That's right, Holmes. Alleged. But there is no denying how his Lordship met his demise. The boy crushed his head in badly with a golf club from the man's own bag and did him in with several blows, it seems. You can see the blood stain still remains." The inspector pointed to the red-tainted grass. "He smashed him with a spoon, we believe, three or four times, maybe more. The poor Lordship's face was nearly unrecognizable from the ferocity of the attack. The boy must have been in a frenzy, yes, sir, a frenzy, to administer so many blows."

"To the left side of the head, yes?" asked Holmes.

"'At's right."

"And the club the attacker used was a spoon."

"Yes, sir. The spoon is the one club missing from the bag."

"I see," said Holmes, now observing the bloody grass with a magnifying glass. "Let me ask you, Inspector, why do you think Mr Daley ran back to the caddie master to obtain help?"

"Well, sir," said the inspector, "we believe he thought the suspicion would stray elsewhere if he acted innocent of the crime and reported it hisself. A bright boy, but not bright enough. We have seen similar cases where the perpetrator tried to cover his crime by reporting it. He's as guilty as they come. Threatened the man and then followed through with the deed."

"Mr Daley is right-handed," said Holmes.

"He is, but we have that resolved, sir. We believe Daley followed Lord Fletcher into the woods and waited until the man concentrated on finding his ball and then ambushed him from the front with a blow of the spoon. Once the man had fallen, Daley bludgeoned him several more times."

"Perhaps," said Holmes, "but I am quite certain most ambushes, as you say, would come from behind and not in front, would not you agree, inspector?"

"Not in this case, Holmes. He hit him from the front. No doubt about that. Now. Are we finished here?"

"A moment," said Holmes. He proceeded to observe the grass with great concentration. I suspected he was reenacting the crime by way of the footprints as he had in so many previous cases. After several minutes he asked the inspector, "May I see the body?"

The inspector gestured helplessly with open hands.

"A bit unusual, Holmes, but I suppose it can be arranged. We may be too late, but I believe a trip to the morgue is possible. No next of kin as far as we can ascertain and a good deal of money and land at stake. It seems Fletcher is not who he claimed to be."

"Fascinating," said I. "And who is he, actually?"

"We're not sure. Still looking into the mystery, but it seems Lord Douglas Fletcher just appeared only fifteen years ago in Glasgow, with both money and a new name. It is a puzzling question, but soon solved. Right. Now, off to the morgue."

I must say that in my years as a physician, I had never seen a more gruesome sight than the morbidly disfigured and bloated face of Lord Fletcher, or whomever the impostor upon the coroner's table before us was. I believed even a close relative would have been unable to identify the man. It was quite disturbing.

"And what would you deduce of our murderer from what you see before you, Watson?" asked Holmes.

"Rather gruesome. I would say the pummeling of Lord Fletcher's face was the work of a very angry and determined man. The murderer hated Lord Fletcher quite dearly, I would say."

"Yes, I am in total agreement. The disfigurement of Lord Fletcher's face went well beyond a murder. This, I believe, is vengeance of the worst kind, Inspector. And he was bludgeoned with his own golf club."

"Indeed, he was."

"And have you recovered the murder weapon?"

"We have not found it as of yet, sir."

"I see. You said Lord Fletcher was killed with his own spoon, because it is missing from his quiver."

"That would be bag, Holmes, not quiver," said I.

"Yes, of course. His bag, then."

"That is exactly the case," said the inspector. "The perpetrator, in this case Daley, undoubtedly absconded with the weapon to cover up the deed, but we shall find it either at the golf course or at his residence."

Holmes lit his pipe and sucked deeply in silence. The combination of the pungent tobacco mixed with the decaying Lord Fletcher had a miserable effect on my insides. I excused myself and retired outside to inhale a bit of the clean, cold air the countryside was so famous for. Soon Holmes and Inspector Gregson joined me.

Holmes was examining something miniscule lying in the palm of his hand. After a moment, he peered at it with his magnifying glass.

"Something of interest?" I asked.

"Yes, indeed, Watson," said Holmes. "I noticed a small sliver of wood stuck to a rather ghastly wound on Lord Fletcher's temple and the good Inspector Gregson has given me permission to analyse the evidence back in my laboratory."

"Against the rules and all," said the inspector, "but I would be the first to admit Mr Sherlock Holmes has better analyzing equipment than the Yard. Besides, if it is part of the spoon Daley used on his Lordship, it will be just one more nail in Daley's coffin, when we find where he stashed the weapon."

"Ah, inspector, but the young lad did not stash it, as you say, because I believe he never saw the weapon. Perhaps this small and insignificant splinter will prove that, after all."

Holmes climbed into the carriage and gestured for us to join him.

"Now," said he, "to Blackheath, first, and then Baker Street, for experimentation and scientific hypothesizing. Then back here early tomorrow to solve the case and hand over the true murderer to the inspector."

"I will believe that when I see it," said the inspector.

"And you will," said Holmes. "Oh, and, Inspector, I should like a sample of wood from one of Lord Fletcher's golf clubs today, and then tomorrow I wish to conduct several interviews with employees and members of Royal Blackheath."

"Do as you wish as it is a waste of your time, sir. Just return me the evidence when your tests are complete and inform me of any results that pertain to the case."

We were off in a flash to Royal Blackheath and then to the depot, and a good thing it was, as Mrs Watson dislikes tardiness when she cooks a well-cut piece of lamb. I did not ask Holmes to join us, for I was certain his experiments would keep him from dining at all that night.

It took Mrs Hudson a great deal of time, I fear, to wake Holmes the next morning, as the detective spent most of the previous night experimenting on the two slivers of wood. Holmes bounded down the final three steps of his residence where Inspector Gregson and I met him.

"Good news, my friends," said Holmes.

"And what news would that be, Holmes?" asked the inspector.

"Ah, excellent news, and especially for young Daley." Holmes held out two slivers of wood. "I have here evidence that Lord Fletcher was not murdered with his own golf club."

"How in heaven were you able to deduce that, Holmes?" said I.

"It was a simple experiment, but one I performed numerous times to be sure of the results. I checked for the specific gravity of both the sliver of wood removed from the late Lord Fletcher and the sample from one of his golf clubs. Though similar in appearance, the sample from the golf club tested at .650 which would be in the range of say, a beechwood, whereas the wood sample removed from the wound tested at .760, which would be more consistent with American hickory, which I believe you said is becoming more popular in the sport, Watson."

"Um—yes. I did mention it in our long discussion of the game."

"I don't see how that proves the innocence of Daley," said the inspector. "He could have used a wood of hickory, couldn't he?"

"Unlikely," said Holmes. "Why go to the trouble of retrieving a club from, say, the caddie area, when there were clubs aplenty in Fletcher's bag. Unlikely."

"Yes, well," said the inspector, "that doesn't explain the missing spoon."

"That has me baffled, also," said Holmes. "But I can assure you, wherever it is, it was not used to bludgeon Lord Fletcher. Perhaps he lost it previously, or never had one."

"I suppose that could be the case," said the inspector. "Well, you will have to go without me, Holmes. We are close to finding Fletcher's true identity. Word from Scotland should arrive soon. If you wish to secure Mr Daley's freedom, it will help if you found the true criminal."

"And I shall, Inspector. Come, Watson. Off to find the culprit. I believe he will have in his possession a chipped, hickory wood golf club."

Instead of going directly to Royal Blackheath to search for a marred club, Holmes insisted we visit Daley in the local gaol. What he hoped to gather from the accused I could not surmise. The boy had a worried, somber look upon his face as he sat pensively across from us in a visiting area. A local constable stood nearby. Daley was as handsome as Miss O'Reilly was beautiful. Once wed, I should say they would have quite attractive offspring.

"I had nothing to do with Lord Fletcher's murder," the boy started. "I heard him yell from the thicket and ran to help. He was dead before I pushed through the brush. I lifted his head. It was horrible, Mr Holmes. I ran back right away for help. The caddie master was nearby. There was no delay. And then they arrest me, because someone had heard me say earlier I wished him dead, but I was angry, though it was not in my mind to do him harm. You believe me, sirs, do you not?"

"Yes, of course," said Holmes. "I came only to ask you what happened to Lord Fletcher's spoon."

"The police have already asked, sir. I told them what I will tell you. Lord Fletcher took it with him into the woods, but it was not with him when I found him all—" The boy held his head in his hands.

"Now, now, lad. You need not worry. The lovely Miss O'Reilly has brought me to your rescue, and that is what Dr Watson and I intend to do."

"How is Mary? They only let me see her the one time."

"She is admirable," said I. "Soon, we will have her in your arms."

"Oh, thank you, sir, and you, Mr Holmes."

We said our goodbyes and took a hansom to the golf club. There, in the caddie house, the master allowed us to inspect the members' golf clubs. Holmes found the murder weapon almost immediately. He held it out to me.

"Hickory, Watson. Notice the small chip of wood missing." He placed the sliver of wood removed from the late Lord Fletcher over the bare spot. It fit perfectly. "And it is a left-handed club, as I expected."

I could not see his reasoning so I asked him to explain.

"Ah. You see, if Lord Fletcher were ambushed from behind, as I expected, then the murderer would have directed the blow to the left side of the face. Since the wounds were not concave in nature, the strike would have to come from the flat surface of this golf club, and thus it would have to be a left-handed club wielded by a left-handed man."

We walked directly to the caddie master.

"May I ask whose bag that is?" asked Holmes.

"That belongs to Mr Arthur Andrews, sir, a member for thirty years now and one of the Nine Hole League."

"Nine Hole League?" I asked.

"Yes, sir. Seven, excuse me, six gentlemen who play only nine holes on the weekend, being their ages are a bit up there. Some are in their eighties, gentlemen."

"You said seven, at first," said Holmes.

"Yes, sir. I forgot Lord Fletcher. He was a member, also the youngest of them all, but no other league would have him because of his confrontational manner and, of course, the accusations."

"Cheating," said I.

"Oh, yes, sir. Quite a bit."

"Thank you," Holmes said, handing him a crown. "May we borrow this club for a short time?"

"It's not mine to give, sir."

"We will ask Mr Andrews then."

"I would appreciate that."

We strode away, club in hand.

"Oh, sir?" asked the caddie master.

"Yes."

"The Nine Hole League. They are in the Rose Room now. Meeting, as they do, for tea."

"Thank you," said Holmes, and we walked briskly towards the clubhouse, to the Rose Room. Soon, we were there. The six men remained seated and looked our way as one.

"Gentlemen. I am Sherlock Holmes and this is my associate, Dr Watson. May I ask which one of you is Andrews?"

A man of, say, sixty or sixty-five stood. "I am he. And what may we do for you? We are having a private meeting."

"You may tell me if this club belongs to you." Holmes held it in front of him.

"It is mine," said Andrews.

"Yes. It is, indeed," said Holmes. He pointed at seven portraits adorning the wall. "I assume these are all the members of the Nine Hole League?"

"They are," said Andrews.

Holmes walked over to the wall. He stopped sharply and stared at one, in particular. Several seconds went by, but Holmes did not move. Somewhat embarrassed, I touched his shoulder. Startled, he turned quickly to me.

"What is it, Holmes?"

"Lord Fletcher," said he. Holmes's face seemed drained of blood and he displayed an almost frightened expression. I was most concerned.

"Yes, Mr Holmes," said Andrews, "that is the bastard. I do not wish God to rest his soul. And I do not regret my actions, except that an innocent man was charged with my crime."

I was not sure Holmes heard any of it as he had turned back to stare, once again, at Lord Fletcher's portrait. Soon I had Holmes sitting and taking tea. When he spoke, his tone and demeanour were that of one bereaved. What in that portrait had changed him?

"It was not you alone who plotted this," said Holmes to Andrews.

An older man spoke. "I am Lord Castor. You know Andrews. The rest of these gentlemen are Messrs. Wallace, Baker, Branigan, and Smyth. Yes, we are all guilty of conspiring."

Holmes looked up from his tea.

"I knew you were all involved. The footprints at the crime scene. Some of course belonged to the police, but the others were indented by shoes with nail pegs similar to what you gentlemen use on the golf course. Would you like to explain to Watson, or shall I?"

Andrews spoke.

"The man was a cretin. When he first joined our league, he bullied his way to be in charge of our group. He cheated and lied at every turn, making it miserable for the rest of us. Without the other members' permission, the man gave our tee time away to another group, which left us with an early morning start. We are too old to play at such an hour and the cold air would surely affect our health. The management refused to expel Lord Fletcher, so we took it upon ourselves to have him thrown out of Blackheath. He then threated to *Buy the damned club*, as he said, and have *us* thrown out. The final straw was when he bullied Smyth." Andrews pointed to the one among them who I believe was the oldest and frailest of the League. "Lord Castor and I served under Captain Smyth in the Crimean and we would let no man bully him. I challenged Fletcher and demanded an apology. The man laughed and slapped me to the ground. I could not let that lay, gentlemen, and so with the help of the others, we concocted our plan."

"Murder," said I.

"Yes. And it was too good for him."

Holmes stood suddenly and spoke.

"So one of you gentlemen would lie in wait on the eleventh, in the expectation Lord Fletcher would hit once again into the woods. I observed from the number of golf shoes that you took turns waiting for the ambush."

Andrews spoke. "It happened to be my turn and when the opportunity arrived, and he was in a position of vulnerability, I struck him four times with my brassie."

"And what of Fletcher's spoon?" I asked.

"I took it with me, hoping the police would assume it the murder weapon. We are very sorry for young Daley's predicament. This meeting today was to come to a consensus and admit the crime so that the boy would be set free. We are old and have lived well. He is but young and with an unknown future, lest we free him."

Holmes's expression did not change, remorseful as it was.

"I would suggest you not admit the crime to the police, gentlemen. Mr Daley will be set free on my evidence alone. The police will search here for the murderer, though they may not look for gentlemen of your status to be the perpetrators. Now, how well do you know this caddie master? Can he be trusted?"

"Jenkins?" asked Andrews. "He is loyal to a fault. I know of no better."

"I see," said Holmes. "May I ask how much money you gentlemen have with you?"

"Money?' asked Andrews. He looked at the others. "I am not sure, seventy, perhaps a hundred pounds amongst us."

"Then give me what you have and ask no questions. Andrews, I suggest you find another set of clubs to use and you should destroy Fletcher's spoon as soon as possible. Good day, gentlemen."

And with that oration, we left.

We walked quickly to the caddie house where Holmes struck up a conversation with the caddie master, Jenkins. I was some distance from them but still able to discern parts of the conversation. Jenkins nodded frequently, saying to Holmes, "Yes, sir. I never cared for the man," and, "I will dispose of them right away, sir," and, "It will be a joy to have Charlie back, sir." Holmes handed the man the hundred pounds and bid him good day.

Outside the caddie house, I confronted Holmes.

"You would let them not be charged for a crime they freely admit to performing?"

"Yes, Watson. This case is complete. I ask you say nothing to Inspector Gregson or anyone else of this. Let us be sure of Daley's freedom and then return to Baker Street. Please, sir, I suffer a tremendous headache."

Inspector Gregson met with us at the police station. Holmes handed him Andrew's brassie.

"So is this the murder weapon?" asked Gregson.

"It is," said Holmes.

"And may I ask where you gentlemen found it?'

"We found it a some distance from the clubhouse on Footscray Road. We then brought it to you. The splinter I removed from Lord Fletcher's wound fits the scar on the club. Daley is innocent of the murder, Gregson. If he had pummeled Fletcher with the club, the blood would be all about him and not restricted to his hands, and it is unlikely he would travel to Footscray to dispose of the club."

"Yes, Holmes. We have decided to release Daley for the moment though he is still a suspect. There is a matter of some new information surfacing about Lord Fletcher. We still have not determined his true identity, the lead from Scotland a false one, but now it seems his lordship was in great debt to some gentlemen of less than stellar character. We are pursuing that possibility as we speak. I will find the murderer, Holmes, whether he is from Royal Blackheath or the underbelly of London. You can be sure of that, sir."

"Perhaps," said Holmes.

As we traveled home, I wondered again what Holmes had seen in Lord Fletcher's portrait that so troubled him.

✗   ✗   ✗   ✗

18 June, 1892
Baker Street, London

I opened a window to rid the room of that blasted opium odour. Holmes alternately sobbed and puffed on his clay pipe. Was I too late? Was his mind so dramatically altered by the narcotic that he had damaged his brain? I dearly hoped not.

"Tell me, what causes your melancholy?" I asked.

He placed the pipe on the table and held his head in his hands. Then he looked up to me and spoke quietly, his eyes rheumy, purple crescents under them.

"We were very young, Watson. Very young, and in love. Her name was Beatrix and she was my first cousin, but when you are in love, as we were—" Holmes wiped his eyes. "When you were in love, as we were, it did not matter of relations, and yet her father forbade us. I begged elopement, but she would not defy him, despite her declarations of love. She married Erskine McKnight, a brute of a Scot who had some royal tie, and they soon relocated to India, funded exceptionally with Beatrix's dowry.

"Immediately, the letters arrived from her to her father complaining of physical and mental abuse. Before action could be taken, McKnight had killed my love, had beaten her to death in a drunken rage. He was arrested, of course, but soon escaped back to Scotland, under an assumed name it now seems."

"Lord Fletcher," I said.

"The same. I recognised the portrait in the clubhouse. Perhaps—Perhaps I have found vengeance after all."

It occurred to me, then, that my friend's horrible loss may have accounted for his lack of attention to the opposite sex over these years. Holmes lowered his head and sobbed. I placed my hand on his shoulder to comfort him. He held it.

"I loved her so, Watson."

THE SPECKLED BANDANNA

by Hal Charles

I

It was early in April when Kelly Locke woke one morning to find a man, fully dressed, by the side of her bed. She sat up with a start.

"Dad," the usually well-poised anchor for Channel 4's Action News exclaimed, her eyes having focused faster than her brain, "what are you doing here…so early?"

"Very sorry to wake you up, honey, but Mrs. Watson insisted."

Kelly's fox terrier leapt on her bed and began licking her face. "Well, I don't smell smoke, so it can't be a fire."

"It is…of a sort," the sixty-ish Chief of Detectives insisted cryptically. "I know today is your birthday, and we were going to do something special, but I brought by somebody *I* think who needs to talk with you…even if she doesn't. She's waiting now in your living room."

"But I can't see her looking like this."

"Nonsense, she's fully dressed," Matt Locke said with a mischievous chuckle. "And there's one more thing about her I need to tell you." Her father paused long enough for Channel 4 to run a commercial. "I am hopelessly and completely in love with her."

Kelly was glad she wasn't in the studio with the stage manager pointing at her to speak, because she couldn't think of a single thing to say.

"I'm the same way when I get around Helen." Matt Locke laughed. "The words just won't come out."

Shooing her father out of her bedroom, Kelly quickly threw on her favorite sweat suit bearing her alma mater's colors, ran her fingers through her night hair, and headed to her living room to meet "the lovebirds." Helen was admittedly quite beautiful, but what struck Kelly the most was the woman's youth—looking like she had just come from the Summer of Love, the tall blonde in the paisley Boho skirt, pink scoop-neck tee, and speckled bandana must have been forty years younger than her father.

"I'm Helen," said the young woman, who was backlit by the French doors. "I dig your pad." She plopped down in Kelly's favorite overstuffed chair. "Now you need to know where I'm coming from."

"Helen is refreshingly direct," chimed in her father like a Greek chorus.

Kelly smiled, detecting the familiar sweet scent of marijuana emanating from the young woman.

"Actually, I'm terrified," said Helen.

"Perhaps you need to go to the police or a psychiatrist," Kelly volunteered a bit sharply.

"Matt is the police, and he recommended you, though I can't figure why a talking-head news-reader can be helpful, unless you really can channel that Sherlock Holmes guy your dad says you grew up loving so much."

"I met Helen a few weeks ago," Matt quickly interjected, "when I was called in to investigate a break-in at Leatherhead, a music store where she works. We just hit it off and one thing led to another and we started having coffee, then lunches—"

"Having lunch with my dad has terrified you?" Kelly said, intentionally misunderstanding.

"Actually your dad has been wonderful about what's going on with me." Helen crossed her legs and assumed a yoga position in Kelly's favorite chair. "Especially since I no longer have Mom and Dad to turn to."

"What happened to your parents, and how is that related to why you're 'terrified'?"

"They were killed a few years ago in a scuba-diving accident in Aruba."

"Perhaps you've heard of them," added the Chief of Detectives, "Ray and Lottie Moran?"

"No," said Kelly.

"Understandable," snipped Helen, gesturing at the news anchor's outfit. "They would never have stooped to making leisure-wear." She looked away from Kelly's sweat suit. "Since their accident, I've been living with my Uncle Henry in the country, which is a real drag because he controls my trust fund until I turn twenty-five next month."

"And you're terrified of all that money?" snipped Kelly.

Helen stood straight up. "I am terrified I will not reach my twenty-fifth birthday."

"Easy," said Matt Locke, his hand on her shoulder. "Helen has been in several near-accidents recently."

Helen hugged her protector. "My junker's brakes failed last week. Then that garbage truck nearly hit me in the mall parking lot. Oh, and I detected the smell of gas coming from the kitchen and had to call the utilities company. They said I was lucky I didn't go inside and turn on something electric."

"Don't forget your amp," reminded the Chief of Detectives.

"Your amp?" said Kelly.

"I play guitar in this retro-rock group, The Stoners, and one day down at the warehouse where we rehearse it shorted out on me. Then there's my ex, M.C. Snake Smith. When we broke up last week, he said I'd regret rejecting him."

"Rock and real relationships go together like oil and water," admitted Kelly.

"Oh," said Helen, "you play and sing, too?"

"No, Yoko, I can just imagine," said Kelly.

"Girl, you don't know the half of it. Listen, we have a rehearsal tonight at the warehouse. Why don't you come by? You could meet the others and see where I was almost done in. Please."

Kelly took one look at the shaking young woman clinging to her father. She was either truly troubled or the greatest actress since Irene Adler. "Why not?"

II

Following directions, Kelly arrived at the semi-abandoned Warehouse of India just before 8:00. As she stepped out of her car, she couldn't help but hear the guitar-heavy, head-banging cacophony of "Magic Carpet Ride." She had to admit the cover sounded very close to the Steppenwolf original.

And there was something else she had to admit, if only to herself. Seeing Helen with her father bothered her. Why, was the question.

Her mother had died a long time ago, certainly long enough for her to have accepted her mom's passing as well as that her father might once again find love.

Inside the warehouse the band had switched to a cover of The Supremes' "You Can't Hurry Love." At least they were versatile performers. She sat down on an old park bench beside her father to watch the five musicians, clustered on a makeshift stage beneath a huge single spotlight. Judging from the butts and broken glass on the cement floor, she decided the building had hosted its share of raves. Just as she was about to talk to her father about her strange feelings, the band broke into The Beatles' "You're Going to Lose That Girl."

Realizing she hadn't ever attended a rock concert with her dad, Kelly shouted, "They're not bad."

"Bad to the bone," he shouted back and added a smile.

The song ended with a few "Yeah, yeahs," and Helen put down her guitar and dragged the keyboard player over. "This is Rocket Givan," she introduced. "He wrote our biggest hit so far, 'Double Run'."

"Which Helen tried to take credit for because she added some lyrics I think she stole from a book jacket."

"You're Kelly Locke. I've seen you on the news," said a short woman in an ASK ME ABOUT MY KIDS sweatshirt. "I got a story for you. 'Lady Rockers Fight Over Snake'."

"I told you, Gypsy Rose," said Helen, "The Beatles have a better chance of getting back together than Snake and I do."

"Back where I come from, you don't say 'I do' unless you mean it," said a tall man with drumsticks, a Tennessee twang, and hair down to his waist.

"This is Squatch Sanders," said Helen. "He's got a thing for me."

"I guess everybody but me does, honey." A male figure wearing a motorcycle jacket with an exotic snake emblazoned on it joined the group. "Helen of Troy, you ain't."

"If I were an interpreter or a psychologist," said Helen, "I'd explain that Snake's trying too hard to say it's been over for us for a long time."

Kelly examined Helen. No, she wasn't of Troy, but her face could launch at least a dozen ships.

"I've got a couple of after-jam dates, so let's get back to rehearsing," said Snake. "But first I gotta go take a smoke."

As he disappeared behind the stage, the other four returned to their instruments. Helen picked up her electric guitar and started to tune it.

Suddenly the huge light in the warehouse went out.

III

When the darkness fell, Kelly's survival instincts took over. She dropped to all fours and, crawling, began retracing her steps into the warehouse. She hadn't noticed the windows blackened when she had first arrived, but they must have been as no light penetrated the room. Unused to pitch darkness, Kelly had a difficult time telling from where the various shouts, some for help and some cursing, originated.

Just as she butted her head against the warehouse door, the light suddenly returned. Across the room the figures resembled a tableau, most frozen in the spot they had been when darkness hit.

"Are you all right, Kelly?" Matt Locke yelled as he spotted her.

"Fine," said the news anchor, disregarding the oil stains that had appeared on her sweat suit.

As her dad grabbed her elbow and led her back toward the group, Kelly let go of her anger and let her thoughts grapple with the pattern she saw emerging.

"No," screamed Gypsy Rose, "it can't be." She pointed to the park bench Kelly had been sitting in. Propped against it was Helen, her eyes closed and a spilt Thermos cup at her side.

"Helen, get up," urged Rocket Givan.

Kelly noticed that his shirt was also wet. Could the same liquid on Helen have been spilled on him?

Squatch Sanders knelt beside the fallen woman and put his fingers to her neck. "I can't feel her pulse."

"Get your hands off her, you filthy pig," screamed Gypsy Rose. "Tonight she was going to come out...and announce we were a couple."

Suddenly Kelly started laughing. It started as a giggle and then she became almost hysterical. Then she turned to her father and jabbed her right index finger in his chest. "It's all your fault, Dad. You caused all this to happen."

Matt Locke stared at his daughter incredulously. Then a broad smile broke across his face. "I confess. Indeed I did it."

Kelly began to circle her father as though she were interrogating a suspect. "I should have figured all this out earlier. I think my mind was clouded by memories of Mom when I should have been thinking more of the moment or in the moment."

Matt Locke looked at his daughter. "What have you and I done every time on the night of your birthday?"

Kelly froze. "Gone out to eat."

"Right," said her father, "so this year I decided to do something special for you, something different."

Helen suddenly sat up in the park bench as though she had been raised from the dead.

Kelly jumped involuntarily.

"When did you know?" prodded her father.

"For a woman whom you've told everyone is the avatar of the Great Detective himself," Kelly admitted, "not as soon as I should have. And the clues were so obvious."

"I'm disappointed," said Helen. "I thought we'd written and produced a great mystery for you, what with all the twisted relationships."

"I told your troupe in the beginning she was a formidable opponent," said Matt Locke.

"A 'real challenge for Mystery Ink' I believe is how you phrased it," said Gypsy Rose.

"No, no," said Kelly. "Helen was really good. I mean, for a while there I really believed she and my dad had a thing going."

"Who's to say we don't?" Matt Locke sat down beside Helen and put his arm around her.

"Dad!" said Kelly.

"So tell me the clues," said Matt Locke, covering his daughter's embarrassment. "I should have known we couldn't fool you."

"Well, the whole day started unusually with you barging into my condo quite early in the morning. Then there was the victim, a terrified woman named Helen who had lost her parents...the reference to Leatherwood...Stoner...India...Helen inheriting her parents' money...Roy and Lottie Moran...Helen's living with her uncle in the country." Kelly looked at the group. "It's Conan Doyle's 'The Speckled Band' with everything but the speckled band—unless you count Helen's bandana."

"Originally we were going to call our supposed rock group The Speckled Band," said Gypsy Rose, "but that seemed too obvious."

"So we settled on the speckled serpent on Snake's motorcycle jacket," said Helen, giving Kelly a hug.

For a split second Kelly caught a whiff of tobacco.

"Speaking of 'Snake'," said Squatch without his Tennessee twang, "where is he?"

"I'll check." Gypsy Rose walked back toward the storage room. Finding the door locked, she stood on her tiptoes and peered through the window. "Helen, oh, my gosh!"

"What is it, Gypsy?" called Squatch.

"It's Snake," replied Gypsy Rose, "and he's sprawled out on the floor not moving and there's blood dripping all over his face."

IV

Kelly turned to her father. "Really, Dad, you didn't have to add more. Act I was an excellent birthday present."

"Kelly," said Matt Locke gravely, "I don't know what you're talking about. As far as I know, this is real."

"It's got to be just another twist in Mystery Ink's script…Act II," argued Kelly.

"Why do you say that?" asked the Chief of Detectives.

"Listen to your little acting troupe. Even though the mystery was supposedly over and they came out of character, they're still calling each other by their noms du guerre—Helen, Snake, Squatch."

"Those," said Rocket Givan, "are our real names."

Matt Locke looked through the bathroom window, then shouldered the door open. Feeling the prostate figure's jugular, he announced, "No pulse." Stubbing out a still-burning cigar, he hurried from the room and pulled out his cellphone. "Locke, badge 1219. I've got a 10-100." Then he gave the warehouse's address and turned to Kelly. "Would I call this one in if it weren't real?"

Kelly glanced at her father's face. The only time she ever saw that determined look was when he was on a case.

Squatch tried to enter the bathroom. Matt Locke pushed him back, then shut the door. "The techs'll be here any minute," he announced. "We've got to keep the crime scene pure."

Kelly's elation quickly turned to chagrin. "I'm sorry...I thought..."

Matt Locke took his daughter aside. "I'm sorry your birthday party and fake murder turned into a real homicide." Then he addressed to the group. "I want everybody on stage. Nobody is leaving."

The players slowly trudged to the platform. Everyone was being quiet until Gypsy Rose suddenly confronted Helen. "You couldn't stand it that he dumped you for another woman, could you?"

Helen jabbed her finger in the woman's chest. "Are you trying to tell me you're the other woman?"

"What if I were?" Gypsy Rose chest-bumped the blonde.

"Then I'd be really upset," said Rocket Givan. "Gypsy Rose and I are together."

"Is that why you and Snake were in each other's face before practice?" said Squatch.

Givan turned on him. "Well, we all know that if anyone needed Snake alive, it was you. I mean, without him you'd have to get a new connection."

Gypsy Rose interrupted. "You got something there, Rocket. Snake's been complaining all night that Squatch is into him for some serious bread, and I don't mean the kind you butter."

"So," concluded Kelly, "it sounds like you all had a motive to turn this quintet into a quartet."

Matt Locke came over to his daughter. "Any ideas?"

As she stood there, she caught a faint whiff of tobacco. "Absolutely."

Kelly asked the four to line up in a single file. Then she walked past Helen, Gypsy Rose, Squatch, and Rocket Givan. In the distance shrilled the nearing sound of police sirens. "Dad," Kelly announced, "arrest Helen. All of them had motive, means, and opportunity, but she's the only one with evidence on her...except you, of course."

"Are you saying I killed my ex-boyfriend?" Helen blurted out.

"What do you mean, except me?" asked the Chief of Detectives.

"When you went into the storage room earlier, Dad," Kelly explained, "I caught a trace of cigar smoke in your hair from the cigar Snake had been smoking, and I know you too well to suspect you'd kill the ex-lover of your new girlfriend."

"Thank you for that confidence," said Matt Locke.

"But earlier I smelled that same scent on one of those four, something I just confirmed. Like you, Helen has the scent trapped in her hair, a scent she is the only one to have, and the only way she could have picked it up was by sneaking into the storage room to kill Snake when the light went out."

"That's kind of flimsy," said Helen smugly. "Besides, by the time the police get here that scent will have disappeared."

"I suspect the techs could still find it, but they won't need to." Kelly pointed at the wet spots on her own sweat suit knees. "Oil. I got it when I started crawling around this warehouse in the darkness. See the wet spot on your clothes, Helen? When I noticed it during Act I, I thought it was poison or something from the thermos beside your body, but I'm betting now it's oil you got when you crawled on the same floor I did, crawled over to the storage room, where you murdered Snake."

"I hated that SOB," confessed Helen. "That self-satisfied smirk on his face really got to me more than it should have."

Matt Locke took out his handcuffs.

"There's just one thing wrong with your theory," said Helen.

"What's that?" said Kelly, certain she had covered everything.

"Me. I'm still alive." A triumphant Snake emerged from the storage room as though he were a leather-jacketed Lazarus.

A bewildered Kelly looked around the warehouse, where the cast of Murder Ink was all smiles.

"You are as good as advertised," said a beaming Matt Locke, handing Helen a check. "Happy birthday again, honey."

"You guys got me," admitted Kelly, hugging her dad.

"The twist of Act II usually does," said the very-alive Snake.

Kelly looked up at her father. "After all those crimes I've helped you solve, I think I needed this come-uppance."

"This wasn't a come-uppance, honey," said her father. "It was a comedy, an attempt to entertain my only daughter and give her the best birthday present ever."

"So this 'relationship' with Helen was also part of the act," guessed Kelly.

"Just like the fake phone call and phony police sirens," said the Chief of Detectives. "Your mother...well, to Matt Locke 'she is always *the* woman'."

THE ADVENTURE OF THE DYING DETECTIVE

by Sir Arthur Conan Doyle

Mrs Hudson, the landlady of Sherlock Holmes, was a long-suffering woman. Not only was her first-floor flat invaded at all hours by throngs of singular and often undesirable characters but her remarkable lodger showed an eccentricity and irregularity in his life which must have sorely tried her patience. His incredible untidiness, his addiction to music at strange hours, his occasional revolver practice within doors, his weird and often malodorous scientific experiments, and the atmosphere of violence and danger which hung around him made him the very worst tenant in London. On the other hand, his payments were princely. I have no doubt that the house might have been purchased at the price which Holmes paid for his rooms during the years that I was with him.

The landlady stood in the deepest awe of him and never dared to interfere with him, however outrageous his proceedings might seem. She was fond of him, too, for he had a remarkable gentleness and courtesy in his dealings with women. He disliked and distrusted the sex, but he was always a chivalrous opponent. Knowing how genuine was her regard for him, I listened earnestly to her story when she came to my rooms in the second year of my married life and told me of the sad condition to which my poor friend was reduced.

"He's dying, Dr Watson," said she. "For three days he has been sinking, and I doubt if he will last the day. He would not let me get a doctor. This morning when I saw his bones sticking out of his face and his great bright eyes looking at me I could stand no more of it. 'With your leave or without it, Mr Holmes, I am going for a doctor this very hour,' said I. 'Let it be Watson, then,' said he. I wouldn't waste an hour in coming to him, sir, or you may not see him alive."

I was horrified for I had heard nothing of his illness. I need not say that I rushed for my coat and my hat. As we drove back I asked for the details.

"There is little I can tell you, sir. He has been working at a case down at Rotherhithe, in an alley near the river, and he has brought this illness back with him. He took to his bed on Wednesday afternoon and has never moved since. For these three days neither food nor drink has passed his lips."

"Good God! Why did you not call in a doctor?"

"He wouldn't have it, sir. You know how masterful he is. I didn't dare to disobey him. But he's not long for this world, as you'll see for yourself the moment that you set eyes on him."

He was indeed a deplorable spectacle. In the dim light of a foggy November day the sick room was a gloomy spot, but it was that gaunt, wasted face staring at me from the bed which sent a chill to my heart. His eyes had the brightness of fever, there was a hectic flush upon either cheek, and dark crusts clung to his lips; the thin hands upon the coverlet twitched incessantly, his voice was croaking and spasmodic. He lay listlessly as I entered the room, but the sight of me brought a gleam of recognition to his eyes.

"Well, Watson, we seem to have fallen upon evil days," said he in a feeble voice, but with something of his old carelessness of manner.

"My dear fellow!" I cried, approaching him.

"Stand back! Stand right back!" said he with the sharp imperiousness which I had associated only with moments of crisis. "If you approach me, Watson, I shall order you out of the house."

"But why?"

"Because it is my desire. Is that not enough?"

Yes, Mrs Hudson was right. He was more masterful than ever. It was pitiful, however, to see his exhaustion.

"I only wished to help," I explained.

"Exactly! You will help best by doing what you are told."

"Certainly, Holmes."

He relaxed the austerity of his manner.

"You are not angry?" he asked, gasping for breath.

Poor devil, how could I be angry when I saw him lying in such a plight before me?

"It's for your own sake, Watson," he croaked.

"For *my* sake?"

"I know what is the matter with me. It is a coolie disease from Sumatra—a thing that the Dutch know more about than we, though they have made little of it up to date. One thing only is certain. It is infallibly deadly, and it is horribly contagious."

He spoke now with a feverish energy, the long hands twitching and jerking as he motioned me away.

"Contagious by touch, Watson—that's it, by touch. Keep your distance and all is well."

"Good heavens, Holmes! Do you suppose that such a consideration weighs with me of an instant? It would not affect me in the case of a stranger. Do you imagine it would prevent me from doing my duty to so old a friend?"

Again I advanced, but he repulsed me with a look of furious anger.

"If you will stand there I will talk. If you do not you must leave the room."

I have so deep a respect for the extraordinary qualities of Holmes that I have always deferred to his wishes, even when I least understood them. But now all my professional instincts were aroused. Let him be my master elsewhere, I at least was his in a sick room.

"Holmes," said I, "you are not yourself. A sick man is but a child, and so I will treat you. Whether you like it or not, I will examine your symptoms and treat you for them."

He looked at me with venomous eyes.

"If I am to have a doctor whether I will or not, let me at least have someone in whom I have confidence," said he.

"Then you have none in me?"

"In your friendship, certainly. But facts are facts, Watson, and, after all, you are only a general practitioner with very limited experience and mediocre qualifications. It is painful to have to say these things, but you leave me no choice."

I was bitterly hurt.

"Such a remark is unworthy of you, Holmes. It shows me very clearly the state of your own nerves. But if you have no confidence in me I would not intrude my services. Let me bring Sir Jasper Meek or Penrose Fisher, or any of the best men in London. But someone you *must* have, and that is final. If you think that I am going to stand here and see you die without either helping you myself or bringing anyone else to help you, then you have mistaken your man."

"You mean well, Watson," said the sick man with something between a sob and a groan. "Shall I demonstrate your own ignorance? What do you know, pray, of Tapanuli fever? What do you know of the black Formosa corruption?"

"I have never heard of either."

"There are many problems of disease, many strange pathological possibilities, in the East, Watson." He paused after each sentence to collect his failing strength. "I have learned so much during some recent researches which have a medico-criminal aspect. It was in the course of them that I contracted this complaint. You can do nothing."

"Possibly not. But I happen to know that Dr Ainstree, the greatest living authority upon tropical disease, is now in London. All remonstrance is useless, Holmes, I am going this instant to fetch him." I turned resolutely to the door.

Never have I had such a shock! In an instant, with a tiger-spring, the dying man had intercepted me. I heard the sharp snap of a twisted key. The next moment he had staggered back to his bed, exhausted and panting after his one tremendous outflame of energy.

"You won't take the key from me by force, Watson, I've got you, my friend. Here you are, and here you will stay until I will otherwise. But I'll humour you." (All this in little gasps, with terrible struggles for breath between.) "You've only my own good at heart. Of course I know that very well. You shall have your way, but give me time to get my strength. Not now, Watson, not now. It's four o'clock. At six you can go."

"This is insanity, Holmes."

"Only two hours, Watson. I promise you will go at six. Are you content to wait?"

"I seem to have no choice."

"None in the world, Watson. Thank you, I need no help in arranging the clothes. You will please keep your distance. Now, Watson, there is one other condition that I would make. You will seek help, not from the man you mention, but from the one that I choose."

"By all means."

"The first three sensible words that you have uttered since you entered this room, Watson. You will find some books over there. I am somewhat exhausted; I wonder how a battery feels when it pours electricity into a non-conductor? At six, Watson, we resume our conversation."

But it was destined to be resumed long before that hour, and in circumstances which gave me a shock hardly second to that caused by his spring to the door. I had stood for some minutes looking at the silent figure in the bed. His face was almost covered by the clothes and he appeared to be asleep. Then, unable to settle down to reading, I walked slowly round the room, examining the pictures of celebrated criminals with which every wall was adorned. Finally, in my aimless perambulation, I came to the mantelpiece. A litter of pipes, tobacco-pouches, syringes, penknives, revolver-cartridges, and other debris was scattered over it. In the midst of these was a small black and white ivory box with a sliding lid. It was a neat little thing, and I had stretched out my hand to examine it more closely, when—

It was a dreadful cry that he gave—a yell which might have been heard down the street. My skin went cold and my hair bristled at that horrible scream. As I turned I caught a glimpse of a convulsed face and frantic eyes. I stood paralyzed, with the little box in my hand.

"Put it down! Down, this instant, Watson—this instant, I say!" His head sank back upon the pillow and he gave a deep sigh of relief as I replaced the box upon the mantelpiece. "I hate to have my things touched, Watson. You know that I hate it. You fidget me beyond endurance. You, a doctor—you are enough to drive a patient into an asylum. Sit down, man, and let me have my rest!"

The incident left a most unpleasant impression upon my mind. The violent and causeless excitement, followed by this brutality of speech, so far removed from his usual suavity, showed me how deep was the disorganization of his mind. Of all ruins, that of a noble mind is the most deplorable. I sat in silent dejection until the stipulated time had passed. He seemed to have been watching the clock as well as I, for it was hardly six before he began to talk with the same feverish animation as before.

"Now, Watson," said he. "Have you any change in your pocket?"

"Yes."

"Any silver?"

"A good deal."

"How many half-crowns?"

"I have five."

"Ah, too few! Too few! How very unfortunate, Watson! However, such as they are you can put them in your watchpocket. And all the rest of your money in your left trouser pocket. Thank you. It will balance you so much better like that."

This was raving insanity. He shuddered, and again made a sound between a cough and a sob.

"You will now light the gas, Watson, but you will be very careful that not for one instant shall it be more than half on. I implore you to be careful, Watson. Thank you, that is excellent. No, you need not draw the blind. Now you will have the kindness to place some letters and papers upon this table within my reach. Thank you. Now some of that litter from the mantelpiece. Excellent, Watson! There is a sugar-tongs there. Kindly raise that small ivory box with its assistance. Place it here among the papers. Good! You can now go and fetch Mr Culverton Smith, of 13 Lower Burke Street."

To tell the truth, my desire to fetch a doctor had somewhat weakened, for poor Holmes was so obviously delirious that it seemed dangerous to leave him. However, he was as eager now to consult the person named as he had been obstinate in refusing.

"I never heard the name," said I.

"Possibly not, my good Watson. It may surprise you to know that the man upon earth who is best versed in this disease is not a medical man, but a planter. Mr Culverton Smith is a well-known resident of Sumatra, now visiting London. An outbreak of the disease upon his plantation, which was distant from medical aid, caused him to study it himself, with some rather far-reaching consequences. He is a very methodical person, and I did not desire you to start before six, because I was well aware that you would not find him in his study. If you could persuade him to come here and give us the benefit of his unique experience of this disease, the investigation of which has been his dearest hobby, I cannot doubt that he could help me."

I gave Holmes's remarks as a consecutive whole and will not attempt to indicate how they were interrupted by gaspings for breath and those clutchings of his hands which indicated the pain from which he was suffering. His appearance had changed for the worse during the few hours that I had been with him. Those hectic spots were more pronounced, the eyes shone more brightly out of darker hollows, and a cold sweat glimmered upon his brow. He still retained, however, the jaunty gallantry of his speech. To the last gasp he would always be the master.

"You will tell him exactly how you have left me," said he. "You will convey the very impression which is in your own mind—a dying man—a dying and delirious man. Indeed, I cannot think why the whole bed of the ocean is not one solid mass of oysters, so prolific the creatures seem. Ah, I am wandering! Strange how the brain controls the brain! What was I saying, Watson?"

"My directions for Mr Culverton Smith."

"Ah, yes, I remember. My life depends upon it. Plead with him, Watson. There is no good feeling between us. His nephew, Watson—I had suspicions of foul play and I allowed him to see it. The boy died horribly. He has a grudge against me. You will soften him, Watson. Beg him, pray him, get him here by any means. He can save me—only he!"

"I will bring him in a cab, if I have to carry him down to it."

"You will do nothing of the sort. You will persuade him to come. And then you will return in front of him. Make any excuse so as not to come with him. Don't forget, Watson. You won't fail me. You never did fail me. No doubt there are natural enemies which limit the increase of the creatures. You and I, Watson, we have done our part. Shall the world, then, be overrun by oysters? No, no; horrible! You'll convey all that is in your mind."

I left him full of the image of this magnificent intellect babbling like a foolish child. He had handed me the key, and with a happy thought I took it with me lest he should lock himself in. Mrs Hudson was waiting, trembling and weeping, in the passage. Behind me as I passed from the flat I heard Holmes's high, thin voice in some delirious chant. Below, as I stood whistling for a cab, a man came on me through the fog.

"How is Mr Holmes, sir?" he asked.

It was an old acquaintance, Inspector Morton, of Scotland Yard, dressed in unofficial tweeds.

"He is very ill," I answered.

He looked at me in a most singular fashion. Had it not been too fiendish, I could have imagined that the gleam of the fanlight showed exultation in his face.

"I heard some rumour of it," said he.

The cab had driven up, and I left him.

Lower Burke Street proved to be a line of fine houses lying in the vague borderland between Notting Hill and Kensington. The particular one at which my cabman pulled up had an air of smug and demure respectability in its old-fashioned iron railings, its massive folding-door, and its shining brasswork. All was in keeping with a solemn butler who appeared framed in the pink radiance of a tinted electrical light behind him.

"Yes, Mr Culverton Smith is in. Dr Watson! Very good, sir, I will take up your card."

My humble name and title did not appear to impress Mr Culverton Smith. Through the half-open door I heard a high, petulant, penetrating voice.

"Who is this person? What does he want? Dear me, Staples, how often have I said that I am not to be disturbed in my hours of study?"

There came a gentle flow of soothing explanation from the butler.

"Well, I won't see him, Staples. I can't have my work interrupted like this. I am not at home. Say so. Tell him to come in the morning if he really must see me."

Again the gentle murmur.

"Well, well, give him that message. He can come in the morning, or he can stay away. My work must not be hindered."

I thought of Holmes tossing upon his bed of sickness and counting the minutes, perhaps, until I could bring help to him. It was not a time to stand upon ceremony. His life depended upon my promptness. Before the apologetic butler had delivered his message I had pushed past him and was in the room.

With a shrill cry of anger a man rose from a reclining chair beside the fire. I saw a great yellow face, coarse-grained and greasy, with heavy, double-chin, and two sullen, menacing grey eyes which glared at me from under tufted and sandy brows. A high bald head had a small velvet smoking-cap poised coquettishly upon one side of its pink curve. The skull was of enormous capacity, and yet as I looked down I saw to my amazement that the figure of the man was small and frail, twisted in the shoulders and back like one who has suffered from rickets in his childhood.

"What's this?" he cried in a high, screaming voice. "What is the meaning of this intrusion? Didn't I send you word that I would see you to-morrow morning?"

"I am sorry," said I, "but the matter cannot be delayed. Mr Sherlock Holmes—"

The mention of my friend's name had an extraordinary effect upon the little man. The look of anger passed in an instant from his face. His features became tense and alert.

"Have you come from Holmes?" he asked.

"I have just left him."

"What about Holmes? How is he?"

"He is desperately ill. That is why I have come."

The man motioned me to a chair, and turned to resume his own. As he did so I caught a glimpse of his face in the mirror over the mantelpiece. I could have sworn that it was set in a malicious and abominable smile. Yet I persuaded myself that it must have been some nervous contraction which I had surprised, for he turned to me an instant later with genuine concern upon his features.

"I am sorry to hear this," said he. "I only know Mr Holmes through some business dealings which we have had, but I have every respect for his talents and his character. He is an amateur of crime, as I am of disease. For him the villain, for me the microbe. There are my prisons," he continued, pointing to a row of bottles and jars which stood upon a side table. "Among those gelatine cultivations some of the very worst offenders in the world are now doing time."

"It was on account of your special knowledge that Mr Holmes desired to see you. He has a high opinion of you and thought that you were the one man in London who could help him."

The little man started, and the jaunty smoking-cap slid to the floor.

"Why?" he asked. "Why should Mr Homes think that I could help him in his trouble?"

"Because of your knowledge of Eastern diseases."

"But why should he think that this disease which he has contracted is Eastern?"

"Because, in some professional inquiry, he has been working among Chinese sailors down in the docks."

Mr Culverton Smith smiled pleasantly and picked up his smoking-cap.

"Oh, that's it—is it?" said he. "I trust the matter is not so grave as you suppose. How long has he been ill?"

"About three days."

"Is he delirious?"

"Occasionally."

"Tut, tut! This sounds serious. It would be inhuman not to answer his call. I very much resent any interruption to my work, Dr Watson, but this case is certainly exceptional. I will come with you at once."

I remembered Holmes's injunction.

"I have another appointment," said I.

"Very good. I will go alone. I have a note of Mr Holmes's address. You can rely upon my being there within half an hour at most."

It was with a sinking heart that I reentered Holmes's bedroom. For all that I knew the worst might have happened in my absence. To my enormous relief, he had improved greatly in the interval. His appearance was as ghastly as ever, but all trace of delirium had left him and he spoke in a feeble voice, it is true, but with even more than his usual crispness and lucidity.

"Well, did you see him, Watson?"

"Yes; he is coming."

"Admirable, Watson! Admirable! You are the best of messengers."

"He wished to return with me."

"That would never do, Watson. That would be obviously impossible. Did he ask what ailed me?"

"I told him about the Chinese in the East End."

"Exactly! Well, Watson, you have done all that a good friend could. You can now disappear from the scene."

"I must wait and hear his opinion, Holmes."

"Of course you must. But I have reasons to suppose that this opinion would be very much more frank and valuable if he imagines that we are alone. There is just room behind the head of my bed, Watson."

"My dear Holmes!"

"I fear there is no alternative, Watson. The room does not lend itself to concealment, which is as well, as it is the less likely to arouse suspicion. But just there, Watson, I fancy that it could be done." Suddenly he sat up with a rigid intentness upon his haggard face. "There are the wheels, Watson. Quick, man, if you love me! And don't budge, whatever happens—whatever happens, do you hear? Don't speak! Don't move! Just listen with all your ears." Then in an instant his sudden access of strength departed, and his masterful, purposeful talk droned away into the low, vague murmurings of a semi-delirious man.

From the hiding-place into which I had been so swiftly hustled I heard the footfalls upon the stair, with the opening and the closing of the bedroom door. Then, to my surprise, there came a long silence, broken only by the heavy breathings and gaspings of the sick man. I could imagine that our visitor was standing by the bedside and looking down at the sufferer. At last that strange hush was broken.

"Holmes!" he cried. "Holmes!" in the insistent tone of one who awakens a sleeper. "Can't you hear me, Holmes?" There was a rustling, as if he had shaken the sick man roughly by the shoulder.

"Is that you, Mr Smith?" Holmes whispered. "I hardly dared hope that you would come."

The other laughed.

"I should imagine not," he said. "And yet, you see, I am here. Coals of fire, Holmes—coals of fire!"

"It is very good of you—very noble of you. I appreciate your special knowledge."

Our visitor sniggered.

"You do. You are, fortunately, the only man in London who does. Do you know what is the matter with you?"

"The same," said Holmes.

"Ah! You recognize the symptoms?"

"Only too well."

"Well, I shouldn't be surprised, Holmes. I shouldn't be surprised if it *were* the same. A bad lookout for you if it is. Poor Victor was a dead man on the fourth day—a strong, hearty young fellow. It was certainly, as you said, very surprising that he should have contracted an out-of-the-way Asiatic disease in the heart of London—a disease, too, of which I had made such a very special study. Singular coincidence, Holmes. Very smart of you to notice it, but rather uncharitable to suggest that it was cause and effect."

"I knew that you did it."

"Oh, you did, did you? Well, you couldn't prove it, anyhow. But what do you think of yourself spreading reports about me like that, and then crawling to me for help the moment you are in trouble? What sort of a game is that—eh?"

I heard the rasping, laboured breathing of the sick man. "Give me the water!" he gasped.

"You're precious near your end, my friend, but I don't want you to go till I have had a word with you. That's why I give you water. There, don't slop it about! That's right. Can you understand what I say?"

Holmes groaned.

"Do what you can for me. Let bygones be bygones," he whispered. "I'll put the words out of my head—I swear I will. Only cure me, and I'll forget it."

"Forget what?"

"Well, about Victor Savage's death. You as good as admitted just now that you had done it. I'll forget it."

"You can forget it or remember it, just as you like. I don't see you in the witnessbox. Quite another shaped box, my good Holmes, I assure you. It matters nothing to me that you should know how my nephew died. It's not him we are talking about. It's you."

"Yes, yes."

"The fellow who came for me—I've forgotten his name—said that you contracted it down in the East End among the sailors."

"I could only account for it so."

"You are proud of your brains, Holmes, are you not? Think yourself smart, don't you? You came across someone who was smarter this time. Now cast your mind back, Holmes. Can you think of no other way you could have got this thing?"

"I can't think. My mind is gone. For heaven's sake, help me!"

"Yes, I will help you. I'll help you to understand just where you are and how you got there. I'd like you to know before you die."

"Give me something to ease my pain."

"Painful, is it? Yes, the coolies used to do some squealing towards the end. Takes you as cramp, I fancy."

"Yes, yes; it is cramp."

"Well, you can hear what I say, anyhow. Listen now! Can you remember any unusual incident in your life just about the time your symptoms began?"

"No, no; nothing."

"Think again."

"I'm too ill to think."

"Well, then, I'll help you. Did anything come by post?"

"By post?"

"A box by chance?"

"I'm fainting—I'm gone!"

"Listen, Holmes!" There was a sound as if he was shaking the dying man, and it was all that I could do to hold myself quiet in my hiding-place. "You must hear me. You *shall* hear me. Do you remember a box—an ivory box? It came on Wednesday. You opened it—do you remember?"

"Yes, yes, I opened it. There was a sharp spring inside it. Some joke—"

"It was no joke, as you will find to your cost. You fool, you would have it and you have got it. Who asked you to cross my path? If you had left me alone I would not have hurt you."

"I remember," Holmes gasped. "The spring! It drew blood. This box—this on the table."

"The very one, by George! And it may as well leave the room in my pocket. There goes your last shred of evidence. But you have the truth now, Holmes, and you can die with the knowledge that I killed you. You knew too much of the fate of Victor Savage, so I have sent you to share it. You are very near your end, Holmes. I will sit here and I will watch you die."

Holmes's voice had sunk to an almost inaudible whisper.

"What is that?" said Smith. "Turn up the gas? Ah, the shadows begin to fall, do they? Yes, I will turn it up, that I may see you the better." He crossed the room and the light suddenly brightened. "Is there any other little service that I can do you, my friend?"

"A match and a cigarette."

I nearly called out in my joy and my amazement. He was speaking in his natural voice—a little weak, perhaps, but the very voice I knew. There was a long pause, and I felt that Culverton Smith was standing in silent amazement looking down at his companion.

"What's the meaning of this?" I heard him say at last in a dry, rasping tone.

"The best way of successfully acting a part is to be it," said Holmes. "I give you my word that for three days I have tasted neither food nor drink until you were good enough to pour me out that glass of water. But it is the tobacco which I find most irksome. Ah, here *are* some cigarettes." I heard the striking of a match. "That is very much better. Halloa! halloa! Do I hear the step of a friend?"

There were footfalls outside, the door opened, and Inspector Morton appeared.

"All is in order and this is your man," said Holmes.

The officer gave the usual cautions.

"I arrest you on the charge of the murder of one Victor Savage," he concluded.

"And you might add of the attempted murder of one Sherlock Holmes," remarked my friend with a chuckle. "To save an invalid trouble, Inspector, Mr Culverton Smith was good enough to give our signal by turning up the gas. By the way, the prisoner has a small box in the right-hand pocket of his coat which it would be as well to remove. Thank you. I would handle it gingerly if I were you. Put it down here. It may play its part in the trial."

There was a sudden rush and a scuffle, followed by the clash of iron and a cry of pain.

"You'll only get yourself hurt," said the inspector. "Stand still, will you?" There was the click of the closing handcuffs.

"A nice trap!" cried the high, snarling voice. "It will bring YOU into the dock, Holmes, not me. He asked me to come here to cure him. I was sorry for him and I came. Now he will pretend, no doubt, that I have said anything which he may invent which will corroborate his insane suspicions. You can lie as you like, Holmes. My word is always as good as yours."

"Good heavens!" cried Holmes. "I had totally forgotten him. My dear Watson, I owe you a thousand apologies. To think that I should have overlooked you! I need not introduce you to Mr

Culverton Smith, since I understand that you met somewhat earlier in the evening. Have you the cab below? I will follow you when I am dressed, for I may be of some use at the station.

"I never needed it more," said Holmes as he refreshed himself with a glass of claret and some biscuits in the intervals of his toilet. "However, as you know, my habits are irregular, and such a feat means less to me than to most men. It was very essential that I should impress Mrs Hudson with the reality of my condition, since she was to convey it to you, and you in turn to him. You won't be offended, Watson? You will realize that among your many talents dissimulation finds no place, and that if you had shared my secret you would never have been able to impress Smith with the urgent necessity of his presence, which was the vital point of the whole scheme. Knowing his vindictive nature, I was perfectly certain that he would come to look upon his handiwork."

"But your appearance, Holmes—your ghastly face?"

"Three days of absolute fast does not improve one's beauty, Watson. For the rest, there is nothing which a sponge may not cure. With vaseline upon one's forehead, belladonna in one's eyes, rouge over the cheek-bones, and crusts of beeswax round one's lips, a very satisfying effect can be produced. Malingering is a subject upon which I have sometimes thought of writing a monograph. A little occasional talk about half-crowns, oysters, or any other extraneous subject produces a pleasing effect of delirium."

"But why would you not let me near you, since there was in truth no infection?"

"Can you ask, my dear Watson? Do you imagine that I have no respect for your medical talents? Could I fancy that your astute judgment would pass a dying man who, however weak, had no rise of pulse or temperature? At four yards, I could deceive you. If I failed to do so, who would bring my Smith within my grasp? No, Watson, I would not touch that box. You can just see if you look at it sideways where the sharp spring like a viper's tooth emerges as you open it. I dare say it was by some such device that poor Savage, who stood between this monster and a reversion, was done to death. My correspondence, however, is, as you know, a varied one, and I am somewhat upon my guard against any packages which reach me. It was clear to me, however, that by pretending that he had really succeeded in his design I might surprise a confession.

That pretence I have carried out with the thoroughness of the true artist. Thank you, Watson, you must help me on with my coat. When we have finished at the police-station I think that something nutritious at Simpson's would not be out of place."